My Teacher's Password

A Contemporary Novel by Jim LaBate

Cover Illustration by Wendy Nooney

Mohawk River Press

Published by
Mohawk River Press
P.O. Box 4095
Clifton Park, New York 12065-0850
518-383-2254
www.MohawkRiverPress.com

This story is fiction. Characters, places, and incidents are either creations of the author or used in a fictional manner. Any similarities to real people, locations, or events are coincidental.

Copyright (Text and Illustration) © 2011 by Jim LaBate
First Printing 2011
Printed in the United States of America
Library of Congress Catalog Card Number: 2011915565
ISBN 9780966210019
10 9 8 7 6 5 4 3 2 1

This book is dedicated to all the people outside my immediate family who have helped me turn my first drafts into final published manuscripts: proofreaders and editors Susan Thayer, Steve Bartholomew, Joe Case, Tim Kelly, and Naomi Ingalls; typesetters Dennis Donohue and Beth Rider; and artists Jeff Mosher, Brian Bateman, and Wendy Nooney.

Other works by Jim LaBate

Let's Go, Gaels – A Novella

Mickey Mantle Day in Amsterdam – Another Novella

Things I Threw in the River: The Story of One Man's Life

Popeye Cantfield – A Full-Length Play

Monday, November 1

A Chinese proverb says that "a 1,000-mile journey begins with a single step." No kidding!

And an American college writing instructor says that "a 50,000-word novel begins with a single word." And that word is "crazy." Or maybe "ridiculous." Or "insane." Choose any one of the above.

Seriously, it's 11:00 on Monday morning, November 1, 2010, and I am supposed to write approximately 1,700 words before I leave this computer classroom today. The teacher for my Creative Writing class, Ms. Cavellari, is encouraging us all to participate in this online project that helps interested writers compose a novel in a month. The basic idea is that we will write a 50,000-word novel before the month is over. She says that's about 1,700 words a day or about five to six pages, double spaced and using a 12-point font.

The pessimistic and sarcastic part of me doesn't want to do this because I'm estimating that it will take me about one to two hours per day just to type that much text. And who knows how much longer it will take me to think of that much text to write in the first place? The optimistic and idealistic part of me, though, knows that this is exactly what I need if I really want to work as a writer someday.

Fortunately, we don't have to do it – the whole thing, that is. We just have to write 1,700 words today. Then, if we want to continue we may, but she's not going to force us, and she's not making this task part of our final grade. And she's actually prepared us quite well to begin.

She forces us to write at least one sentence in our journals every day, and she says that if we can write that first sentence, the odds are good that we will keep going. And she's right about that. Since we began during the first week of class, I've increased my daily writing from three or four sentences to at least a page a day. So, here goes.

My name is Tom Sullivan. I'm a junior at Kennedy College near Albany, New York. I graduated from Albany Community College (ACC) last spring, and I am actually living on a college campus now for the first time. Since my parents couldn't afford to send me away to college for four years, they said I could live on campus for my junior and senior years if I first proved that I was serious about college by graduating from a two-year school. At that time, I assumed I'd go far away for college, but now I'm pretty happy to stay in the area because I've visited a lot of my friends at their schools, and I like the fact that I know this area so well. I don't have a strong desire to live in New York City or Buffalo or Syracuse, and moving to another smaller area just to be away from home doesn't really make a lot of sense. So I'm staying near home but living in the dorms at Kennedy and enjoying myself.

My roommate, Teddy, is also a transfer student, but he's from downstate, and he's really serious about his education, so I don't even really see him that much. He's a business major, and he always goes to the library to study, so in some ways, I feel like I have a single room.

My favorite part about living in the dorms, though, is the cafeteria. Most of the guys who have been here for a while are always complaining about the food, but I haven't reached that point yet. I love the fact that I can just walk over there and eat pretty much whenever I feel like it. I don't have to shop for food, I don't have to cook, and I don't have to clean up. Does it get any better than that? I think I'll keep living on campus even after I graduate and get married.

Actually, however, now that I think about it, the food is only my second favorite part. I love being on campus with all these beautiful girls. We had a lot of good-looking girls at ACC, too, but there's a little something extra about having them on campus all the time. Usually, at ACC, I'd only see the girls during the daytime; here, I get to also see them in the morning before classes when they stop in the cafeteria for breakfast, and I get to see them again at the end of the day for supper, and then I get to see them at night, too, when they're working out at the gym or swimming in the pool or even studying in the library. They're just always around, and it's wonderful.

At first, I thought I might feel funny living in a coed dorm because I was so used to just guys at my house – two older brothers – but now I feel so comfortable walking down all the halls where the girls live. By the way, each floor of each dormitory is either all male or all female, and Teddy and I are on the fifth floor of a wing that looks out over the baseball field.

So anyway, getting back to this whole novel-in-a-month thing, Ms. Cavellari says we don't even need a story to begin this project. She says we just have to keep writing as quickly as we can, and we don't have to worry about character or plot or anything. She just wants us to write without stopping until we get to our daily word count of 1,667. She says that most writers spend too much time thinking and not enough time writing, so this is her way of forcing us to get started. She claims that eventually, something will trigger a story for us, and we'll really start writing once we hit that point. In the beginning, however, she just wants us to write and watch the words add up. At this moment, though, I'm a little skeptical, and my fingers are starting to get tired. I think I may already be suffering from carpal tunnel syndrome.

I signed up for this course because I do like to write, and I need someone to push me. I have lots of vague ideas for stories, but I don't know where to go with them. So far, this course has been pretty good because Ms. Cavellari has already had us write some character sketches, a bunch of poems, and a short story. She even said we could incorporate some of those things into this project if we wanted to, but I'm not feeling it yet.

So let me tell you about Ms. Cavellari. I think I may have a crush on her. Okay, I definitely have a crush on her. She's probably in her late twenties, she's got long, dark hair, and she's on the thin side but not so thin that she would break. She looks athletic, too, and I know she works out because she talks about going to the gym three mornings a week. That's pretty amazing in itself. In any event, she's adorable. She looks a little like a mixture of Catherine Zeta-Jones, the wife of Michael Douglas, and Penelope Cruz. Okay, probably nobody is as gorgeous as a cross between those two, but Ms. Cavellari has a little bit of both of those two beauties, and she's basically "hot." I have always been attracted to those dark, Italian types, and she definitely fits the mold.

Also, I'm probably in love with her because I've been without a girlfriend for almost two full years. I was dating a girl in high school, and we even stayed together for a while after high school, but we grew tired of each other. We had been in school together since sixth grade, we knew each other's family pretty well, and we got along great, but we were too much like good friends, and we both wanted to see other people, so we agreed to split. Since we split, though, I haven't met anybody that I feel as comfortable with, and she's been dating a new guy that she met at college, so I'm history as far as she's concerned. In reality, I don't want to start dating her again anyway; I would just like to have a girlfriend once in a while to do stuff with. I don't think I want to get locked into a serious relationship because that can be tiresome. So who knows what will happen?

Okay, I just checked my word count, and I'm getting near my quota for the day, so I have to finish strong.

I'm really frustrated by the Jets and their 9-0 loss to the Packers yesterday. The Jets played a lousy game, especially the receivers. They had lots of dropped balls, and the Packers' defenders practically stole two passes away from the Jets' receivers. I think I got spoiled by the Jets' five-game winning streak, and I expected us to cruise for a while. Now, the Patriots are a game ahead. How did that happen?

Okay, I am definitely running out of steam here, and I can't go eat lunch until I finish. Some of my classmates have already left. Quite honestly, I think some of them cut and pasted some stuff they had written previously because I don't ever remember them being that quick. Actually, I've never been this quick before either. Maybe all those forced writing assignments earlier in the semester are paying off. Ms. Cavellari used to make us write for five minutes straight without stopping. That was practically impossible at first; now, I'm pretty good at it. Can I really do this for 30 days? I don't know. I feel like I'm out of words already, and I haven't even finished day one yet. I sometimes wonder how the guys on the radio talk shows do it every day. I listen to them just go on and on about various subjects before they even open up the phone lines, and I'm amazed. Where do they get all that stuff? I don't have that gift of gab. Of course, some of those guys do repeat themselves to fill the air, but the good ones are really good and enjoyable to listen to as well.

So what am I going to do for my career? Good question. I'd like to know the answer to that one as well. Sometimes, I think I might like to be a sportswriter, and at other times, I think it might be too much work for me. I find that I'm not as much of a sports fanatic as I used to be, and I really like to just read novels now, so, who knows, maybe I could be a novelist. I'll let you know for sure at the end of this month. Okay, that's about 1,700 words for today, so that's it. I'll see you again tomorrow.

Tuesday, November 2

It's Tuesday the second, and it's late. I was hoping I'd get to do some of this writing earlier in the day, but, obviously, I didn't. I couldn't even write during class today because our Creative Writing class only meets on Monday, Wednesday, and Friday. Actually, I don't think that matters anyway because we're going back to our normal class activities tomorrow; using Monday's entire 50 minutes, and then some, was just Ms. Cavellari's way of getting us started. But maybe she'll give us some class time on those other days if we finish our regular work early.

So anyway, I didn't get to write earlier today because I went home after classes, so I could vote in the election. School is not that far from home – only 20 minutes – but it's on the other side of the river and in a different election district. I suppose I could have requested an absentee ballot a while back, but that would have required some planning on my part, and, obviously, I didn't think of it. Of course, I could have also blown off the entire election like a lot of guys I know, but I did want to vote. This is the first time I've been able to vote for governor. Plus, just about every teacher I saw today reminded us about how important it is to vote, so I'm glad I did. Did I really know what I was doing? Not exactly. I pretty much voted along party lines. I used to think that was stupid and that I should choose the person rather than the party, but for a combination of reasons, the straight vote worked for me this year.

The trip back home worked out, too, because I was able to do my wash, get a good meal, help Dad with a small project, pick up a few things I needed from the house, and bust my brothers' chops a little bit – all in one trip. We do have washers and dryers in the basement of the dorm, but that requires money and patience. It's so much easier to do the wash at home. Mom always says she won't do it for me, but if I play stupid, which I'm good at, she'll come in and take over. Then, I can watch TV and eat snacks while I wait. What a deal!

And even though I mentioned previously that I really like the food in the cafeteria at school, I still prefer Mom's homemade sauce with spaghetti and meatballs. Mom's side of the family is Italian, and they've been cooking that stuff forever, so it's pretty much perfected by now. Before we ate, however, I had to help Dad replace a portion of the rain gutter over the front door. It came down last winter when we had some huge icicles build up, and we really should have repaired it over the summer, but we typically wait until the last minute for those kinds of tasks, and this was no exception. The whole job only took about an hour. Usually, as the baby of the family, I don't get to do much of that stuff – except maybe go for tools and parts and, then, clean up afterwards – but this time, I was the Big Dog because Dad hurt his foot last week and couldn't climb the ladder and because Matt and Jason were still at work. It felt pretty good, I have to admit, to be able to do the job and get it done. Way to go, Big Guy!

During supper, I also got to tease those guys and Dad because they're all doing so poorly in our online football pool. Every week, the four of us pick all the NFL games, and I am winning big this year. We're only about halfway through the season, and I'm already five games ahead of them. I don't think I've ever been that far ahead of anyone before. They were cool, though. They assume that I've been lucky, which is true, but I'll take it. And since they're all big Giants fans, they had a great time teasing me about the Jets getting shut out. Oh well, we'll have to move on from that one.

So now that I'm back in the dorm, I'm tempted to turn on the TV and watch election results, but I told myself I couldn't until I wrote my 1,700 words.

So what else is new? The San Francisco Giants won the World Series last night. Big deal! I didn't even watch. Once the Mets faded from the race, I pretty much gave up on baseball. Funny, when I was a kid, I thought baseball was so much better than football, and now I feel just the opposite. The baseball games seem to really drag, yet I hate to miss even one play in football. Does that mean I'm growing up in some way? Does that mean I'm maturing? I doubt it.

The weather today was gorgeous. Perfect fall day. The girls were adorable in their flannel shirts and their sweaters. I think the thing I hate most about winter is that the girls have to be so bundled up all the time. It's almost like they're from the Middle East, and all we can see is their eyes. So I'm in no big hurry for winter to come. Again, when I was a kid, I used to enjoy being outside in the snow: sledding, snowball fights, snow forts. Not anymore. The only winter activity I really enjoy is when the first heavy snowfall comes with good packing, and we have a big snowball fight in the neighborhood back home. Of course, I might miss that this year if the first heavy snow comes when I'm on campus. I suppose I can deal with that.

School was actually pretty relaxed today compared to last week. Last week, all of the teachers were giving mid-term exams or requiring major assignments to be turned in because mid-term grades were due; we should get those tomorrow. So yesterday and today, we were back to the basic classroom stuff: lectures and class discussions. In addition to this Creative Writing class, I'm also taking an American History class, a science class, a philosophy class, and a religion class. They're not too bad either. I really enjoy the reading in history and philosophy, and the science isn't as bad as I thought it would be. It's mostly about current controversial issues such as global warming, deforestation, and cloning, that kind of stuff, and not about all that other science that I hate with the periodic table and body parts. And the religion course is probably the easiest one of all because my family's pretty serious about church, and we've been going forever. I even went to a Catholic grade school, so I've heard all of those Bible stories before. I'm pretty sure I have straight B's for my mid-term grades, but I'm also pretty sure that some of them will be A's by the end of the semester; everybody here says that most teachers grade low at the mid-term, so we don't get a big head and start goofing off. I can live with that.

Tomorrow night, I have to work from midnight to 8:00 a.m., in the computer lab at ACC. They have a 24-hour lab over there, and they always need somebody on hand to put paper in the printers and change the ink cartridges and answer general computer questions. Since I had a work-study job over there last year, Frankie, my old supervisor, agreed to let me work one night a week since they couldn't find anybody else. And it's not like I'm a computer geek or anything, but I do know a fair amount about the system and about some of the programs, and since a lot of their students are returning adults who know nothing about computers, I look like a real wizard. They pay me pretty well too: ten bucks an hour, and I can do whatever I want while I'm waiting for people to ask me questions. So some nights, I do my homework, and other nights, I just goof off and play computer games or surf the internet. So actually, Wednesday night will be a good time to write my 1,700 words. I know; technically, if I start at midnight, I will have missed Wednesday completely, but Ms. Cavellari says that our daily word count is just a goal to keep us on track. As long as we average 1,700 words a day for the entire month, we should be okay. Who knows? Maybe I'll get 3,400 words done while I'm over there tomorrow night, and I'll be done for Thursday before the day even begins. Yeah, I'll believe that when I see it.

Actually, the hard part of that job is staying awake all night and, then, also staying awake in classes the next day. Fortunately, I've gotten pretty good at dozing while pretending to read – at work I mean, not in class – so I can catch a few cat naps during the night, especially between three and six when hardly anybody's there. There is one security guy who stops in, though, just to bust my chops. He loves to scare the daylights out of me when I'm dozing. I'll have to come up with something to get even with him one of these days.

Alright, I'm at the home stretch for today, and I hope I discover a plot to this story soon. If I don't, I'm not sure I'll make it. This could be the most boring novel ever written. Maybe I just need to come up with another character or another narrator. I'll have to give that some thought tomorrow.

Wednesday, November 3, and Thursday, November 4

Here I am, finally settled in for my Wednesday work night. Technically, of course, it's Thursday morning because it's 12:45 a.m., and I've been busy since I arrived at midnight. Already, I've had to fix a paper jam in the printer, clean up the mess some students left in the corner of the lab, show one older woman how to do a PowerPoint program, and fix the stapler. I had some nights last year when I didn't work that hard during the entire eight-hour shift. Maybe that means I'll be real busy tonight, and the whole shift will pass quickly. Actually, I hope that's not the case because, first, I don't want to work that hard, and, second, I have to get my 1,700 words in, and, third, and I shouldn't type this too loudly, but I actually have a story to tell, one that is pretty interesting, too. But let me cover some other things before I get into the good stuff.

To begin, the election results were pretty much what everyone expected, at least on the national level. There was a lot of turnover in the House and some in the Senate, though not as much as everyone hoped for. But on the local level, practically all of the incumbents won, which is amazing because all the talk has been about getting rid of the status quo and starting over. In fact, I saw quite a few political signs this year that weren't even for any one candidate but merely said, "Vote Them Out." The talk-show guy that I sometimes hear in the morning was livid. He couldn't control himself he was so mad. And since this particular guy actually owns the radio station, he said he's so frustrated that he might actually move his business to another state with lower taxes and with more support for small businesses.

In history class today, we actually talked about the election, and our teacher said that the subject of national turnover versus local incumbents would make a great research paper, so I might try and do that in the spring when I take my first political science course.

And speaking of other courses, I also got my mid-term grades today, and I predicted them almost perfectly. I got all B's except for, drum roll please, one A in, another drum roll please, a long and loud one, "Creative Writing!" Yes! That means Ms. Cavellari must be in love with me because my grades so far really don't average out to a 90 or above, so she must be feeling something for me. Okay, maybe she likes the fact that I participate all the time and am much more into the whole writing thing than the rest of my classmates. I like the first theory a lot better, though.

Okay, are you ready for the good stuff? A story that might actually evolve into a plot for this silly novel? Yes, I realize that a novel is technically fiction, make believe, but this story could easily be adapted into a fictional piece, and that's what I'm thinking about at the moment. In fact, Ms. Cavellari tells us all the time that "writers write what they know, and fiction writers just change the names, the places, and the times." So here it is.

Whoops, sorry for the interruption. I just had to show one guy how to log into the system. That's unbelievable. We're more than halfway through the semester, and he's just learning how to log into the system! Not looking good for that guy – unless, of course, he's taking one of those "Sprint" courses that double up on classes and run only for the second half of the semester. Like you care about that stuff. "Like you care?" Who am I writing to? I feel like I'm a teenage girl, and I'm writing to my diary. Hey, maybe that's a good thing if it keeps me writing and moving toward my daily word count.

So anyway, wait, let me turn my screen toward the wall a bit more, so nobody can see what I'm actually typing.

Oh my God! Another interruption. The security clown just stopped in, so I had to listen to him complain for ten minutes about what a hard job he has. Give me a break! All he does is walk around the campus with his walkie-talkie and check all the buildings – like that's hard. And like he's qualified to do anything more. He keeps talking about how he has to get a new job because he has to work so many hours each week, but when I ask him where he's going to work, he doesn't have a clue. If he were really smart, which I don't think he is, he'd start taking some actual courses in law enforcement, so he's not still complaining about this job in ten years when he turns 40.

I know. You didn't really need that story on the security guy, but because I'm so focused on trying to get 3,400 words during this shift, I'm taking every opportunity to add to the word count.

Okay, are you finally ready for the big news? You better be because it involves the beautiful Ms. Cavellari!

We were in class today, and as always, I arrived early. I don't arrive early for all my teachers, but I always arrive early for Ms. Cavellari. I was there so early, in fact, that I had to wait for the 10:00 Public Speaking class to finish. As those students started coming out of the classroom, I entered, and I watched as their teacher answered a few questions, closed out of his PowerPoint program on "Powerful Conclusions," and logged out before he exited.

Naturally, as he logged out and prepared to leave, he left the projector on for Ms. Cavellari. She actually arrived a minute or two late, so she apologized and hurriedly logged in herself. That's when it happened.

As she was logging in, pretty much everyone else in the class was absorbed in their own conversations or computer work, but I was watching on the screen behind her, and I saw her type in her user name: m-cavellari. No big deal there; all the teachers have the same basic e-mail address: first initial, hyphen, and last name. Her first name, by the way, is Margaret, and she told us we could call her Margaret if we wanted to, but I just can't bring myself to do it. Must be that Catholic upbringing.

So anyway, because I had nothing else to do, I was still watching her log in, but while rushing, she must not have moved her cursor or hit the tab key, or perhaps she didn't click on the password box before she began typing because her password suddenly appeared in the username box for everyone to see. I was stunned. Obviously, if she had entered her password properly in the appropriate box, the computer would have blacked out her password, so no one could see it, but that didn't happen. I glanced quickly to see if anyone else noticed, and again, everyone was preoccupied, so I turned to my computer and pretended that I hadn't seen what happened. She must have discovered her error quickly because soon enough, she was taking attendance as she waited for her account to open.

I was tempted to write down the password, so I wouldn't forget it, but I realized that wasn't really necessary because her password was so easy to remember: GoPats2002. Even though I hate the New England Patriots, I know that 2002 was their first Super Bowl victory, and I also know that Ms. Cavellari is from Boston – she talks about it all the time – so that password made perfect sense for her. Made perfect sense for me too. I'd never forget it. But as soon as I saw her password, I was a torn man.

My first inclination was to log into the system immediately under her name to see if it worked. And as I thought about it, I figured I could read her e-mail and see what else she had loaded onto her space on the system. But then, the angel on my other shoulder said, "Tom, you can't do that. That would be a violation of her privacy. That would be like breaking into her home and snooping through her stuff."

Good point, I thought. I can't do that. But then the devil in me said, "It's not like breaking in and snooping; it's more like she accidentally left the front door open when she went away for the weekend, so you're simply going in to look around and make sure that everything is okay. This is a good thing you will be doing."

He's a clever guy, that devil. And persuasive too. But not persuasive enough. Even though I was tempted, even though I was curious, and even though I desperately wanted to go into her account, I resisted. Instead, I stayed in my own account where I belonged, and I began doing some of the writing exercises she had prepared for us. She had us write a paragraph in the first-person point of view with the topic sentence at the end. Then, she had us write the same paragraph in the third-person point of view. She is always coming up with these unique assignments to "stretch" our writing abilities. During the actual writing, I temporarily forgot about the temptation, but later, while we were discussing what we had written, I began to daydream.

Most likely, her college e-mail probably wouldn't be that interesting, probably all the same stuff that we get in our student e-mails: announcements about upcoming events, press releases, notices about a broken elevator or water pipe. Boring! And her files would probably be just more of the same stuff she shows us in class: handouts about writing, creative exercises, PowerPoints. No big deal.

But maybe she had pictures in there. Maybe I'd get to see photos of her at the beach on Cape Cod. Would she be wearing a bikini? Now, I was interested. Now, I was tempted again. I knew I couldn't go in there during class, but later, I would have to check it out. I'd have to, no doubt about it.

After class, I actually saw Teddy in the cafeteria, and we had lunch together. I thought about telling him what happened, but I decided against it. He's even more of a straight arrow than I am, so I knew he'd be against the idea, and he'd try to talk me out of it, and I didn't want to be talked out of it at that moment. So after we finished eating, I went to the computer lab in the library. Fortunately, I found an empty computer in the far corner, and I logged in – as myself. As much as I wanted to go into her account, I couldn't pull the trigger, so to speak. I felt guilty. I knew it was wrong. I held off. I felt pretty good about myself too. I figured the initial temptation would be the hardest, and if I could resist early on, I could persevere and ride out the storm. Boy, am I like a cliché machine or what? Ms. Cavellari would not be proud of that. But she would be so proud of my self-control.

Okay, I can't write any more of this tonight. If I do, I will just convince myself to go in there, so I think I'll go to our football pool web site and make my picks for the week.

Friday, November 5

I didn't get up to my Wednesday-Thursday quota at work, so I have to pound out quite a few words today to catch up. Should be easy, though, because guess what? Yes, you got it. I caved in. The temptation never went away, and instead of getting easier to resist, it just got harder. I only have morning classes on Thursday, so I took a nap after lunch, and when I woke up at about 4:00 p.m., I couldn't take it any longer. In fact, I had dreamed about Ms. Cavellari. That's how much I was thinking of her. She and I were rowing a boat together on a big lake, but we kept going in circles. I'm not sure what that means, but it's probably not a good omen.

I was alone in my dorm room and working on my laptop when I logged in. I wasn't worried about being caught or interrupted because I knew the door was locked, and I knew Teddy had classes until late at night. I felt a bit nervous when I keyed in Ms. Cavellari's username and password, but everything worked perfectly.

Since I was really hoping for pictures, I went into her "My Pictures" folder first. Nothing. Well, not nothing exactly, but not much either. She only had three folders of pictures in there: one marked "family," one marked "work," and one marked "miscellaneous." Naturally, I went into the "family" folder first because I was hoping for those bikini photos on the beach. No such luck. She had about a dozen shots in there, and most of them looked like they were taken at somebody's birthday party. She was all dressed up and beautiful, which was nice, and she was standing with what had to be her parents and with some other family members: siblings or cousins, I'm guessing. The two photos that weren't party related looked like they may have been taken at Fenway Park though I couldn't be sure.

Next, I went into the "work" folder, and I was disappointed there too.

Believe it or not, she has pictures of grammatical errors on public signs, things like "Smith and Smith, Certified Pubic Accountants." I'm sure she's collecting them, so she can put them in a PowerPoint program and show them to us in class. Then, of course, we'd have to find the errors. That would actually be somewhat entertaining and fun in class, but again with my high expectations for bikini photos, these pictures were pretty lame by comparison.

Finally, I opened the "miscellaneous" folder and found nothing whatsoever. She must have created the folder just in case she needed one and hadn't yet found anything worthwhile to put in there. What a disappointment.

Fortunately, I still had her e-mail to look forward to. As I mentioned earlier, my expectations weren't too high, but I was curious nonetheless. So when I first started reading her e-mails, they were even more boring than I expected. Not only did she have all the same college announcements that students normally receive, but she also had a ton of short and stupid e-mails from students:

"Dear Ms. Cavellari, What chapter were we supposed to read this week?"

"Ms. Cavellari, I won't be in class today, but I will send you my assignment."

"Ms. Cavellari, Can I have an extra day to finish my essay?"

What a bunch of wimps. Why couldn't they just go to class and do their work on time? I don't think I've ever sent her an e-mail. In fact, I don't think I've ever even spoken to her outside the classroom. I really need to work on that, especially now that I know she has such a crush on me. What a dreamer!

Like a bored fool, though, I kept reading. I was somewhat interested to see which of my classmates – or anybody else I knew for that matter – was writing to her. I noticed that a lot of the girls in our class wrote to her, and a lot of them called her "Margaret" just as she had requested. These e-mails, too, were mostly class related, but they were more on the positive side. Instead of asking for more time for an assignment or explaining why they didn't do something, these girls were really working hard to get an A.

"Margaret, thank you for all the extra help you gave me today during your office hour. I really appreciate your kindness."

"Margaret, if my term paper is a page or two over the required amount, will that be a problem?"

"Margaret, if I send you my research paper early, would you review it and get it back to me before the first draft is due?"

Really? Are you kidding me? Some of that stuff seems over the top. A page or two "over" the required length? Extra help "before" the first draft. These girls are serious. That can't be good for me. What if Ms. Cavellari only gives out a certain number of A's in each class? Does that mean I have to go above and beyond just because these girls are going overboard? They could wreck things for all of us. I'm usually not this hyper about grades, but I do want to get an A in this class. I want to impress Ms. Cavellari with my seriousness, with my writing ability, and with my intelligent comments in class, but maybe I'm out of my league here. I've never felt intimidated by my writing classmates before, but now I'm starting to wonder.

So as I'm reading these e-mails and cursing out these crazy females, my laptop makes that little noise that it always makes when a new e-mail arrives. Like a little girl, I jumped a bit. I wasn't expecting to be interrupted during this sneaky adventure, and at that moment, I felt like I had been caught. I half expected the campus security force to start banging on the door and tell me to come out with my hands in the air.

Once I recovered, I noticed that the e-mail was from Mr. Masterson, another teacher in the English department. I also noticed that it was a forward from a previous e-mail to all the faculty members. Though I was extremely curious to see what he had to say, I also like to read these kinds of e-mails in order, so before I read his recent note, I scrolled down to the message that preceded it.

Apparently, the faculty association is sponsoring a night out on a big river boat that cruises up and down the Hudson River. Though I've never been on one of these cruises, I've heard that they're pretty cool with a lot of dancing and drinking. The cruise was scheduled for Saturday night, November 13, from 7:30 p.m. to midnight, and here's what Mr. Masterson had to say to Ms. Cavellari:

"Margaret,

I know you're new to the area, so I wanted you to know that these riverboat cruises are a lot of fun. If you're interested, I could pick you up and drive you to the pier. Then, we can enjoy the evening with the rest of our colleagues. Think it over, and let me know.

Tony"

Boy is he smooth or what? A little too smooth if you ask me. "Enjoy the evening with colleagues." Who is he kidding? He just wants to get to know the newest and most beautiful faculty member on campus. I didn't really know the guy, but I hadn't heard good things about him. According to Megan, one of my writing classmates, he's been divorced for a while, and some of the girls who have had him for class have implied that he's a bit too friendly with them. I don't get the feeling that he's actually crossed the line with any students, but he's got that look, if you know what I mean.

He has to be close to 50, he uses the comb over to cover up his bald spot, he's out of shape, and he leaves too many of his top shirt buttons undone; like the 20-year-old girls in his class want to see his gold necklace and his hairy chest. I do not have a good feeling about Ms. Cavellari going to this cruise with him.

What should I do? Should I delete the e-mail before she has a chance to see it? Should I try to warn her in person about him? Or maybe I could sabotage the date in some way? Obviously, I was getting too far ahead of myself. Maybe I should just wait to see if she agrees to go with him. If she does, I'll be disappointed, but even if she actually goes with him, what are the chances that she will be at all interested in him? He could be her father, for crying out loud. I couldn't believe it.

So during class on Friday morning, I tried to watch Ms. Cavellari a bit more closely. I wanted to try to determine if she had read Mr. Masterson's e-mail and, perhaps, showed any reaction. If she were extra giggly, that might show that she was interested. Or maybe if she seemed extra confident and outspoken, that might show that she was laughing at him to think that he had any chance with her. As I thought about all that, I realized that she probably wouldn't react in either of those ways. Those are the reactions that I often see in the girls my age when they talk about guys. But Ms. Cavellari is so much more mature than that. I'm sure she's well beyond all that silly high-school stuff. And, in fact, she didn't show any indication in class that anything was different. And class was great too.

First, she showed us a video called "Validation" on YouTube that was really well done and had a clear message about how we should treat other people. The video was only about 15 minutes long, but the acting was great, and so were the settings and the music. Then, after we discussed the video for a while, she said that our next assignment would be to create a short video of our own.

Initially, I thought she was joking, but she was serious. She told us that the English department had recently purchased about 20 or 25 of those small Flip cameras which allow users to record up to one hour of video. And the really neat thing about the cameras is that they have a special attachment that plugs into the computer, so that we can immediately transfer whatever we've filmed. How cool is that! And apparently, once we get the video on the computer, we can use a certain program to edit our film and add sound or pictures or special effects. The whole thing seems really neat. I have no idea at this point what I will film, but we have two to three weeks for the project, so I'm sure I will think of something.

Then, before class ended, she reminded all of us to check our grades online to make sure that all our assignments up to this point have been turned in and recorded. I knew I didn't have any missing assignments, but I logged in anyway and went into the grade book for this class just to check. Sure enough, everything had been submitted and recorded accurately, and I noticed that my numerical average was an 89: technically a B but close enough to an A that she gave me the benefit of the doubt on my mid-term grade. Again, however, I began to wonder how generous she would be at the end of the semester, especially if all those brown-nosing girls were doing all they could to get their own A's. If only I could go back and do over some of my early assignments when I hadn't yet felt comfortable on this campus and when my work wasn't quite as strong as what I was doing now. At that point, I was hit with a bit of divine inspiration. Since I had Ms. Cavellari's username and password to get into the Kennedy College computer system and since I had already been in her computer account, wouldn't that same username and password allow me to get into her teacher's account for the online grading system?

Oh no. The same temptation all over again. The temptation I was able to resist for only a short time. This time, though, I'd really be tempted to cross the line. I felt pretty certain that I could get in there and look at everything, and I also felt pretty certain that I would do so. But could I hold myself back from actually changing a grade. I remember seeing an old movie where a high-school kid hacked into the school's system and changed a grade for his girlfriend, and I imagined it would be just as easy once I got in there. But was it worth it? The evil part of me asked, "What good is it to have the username and password if I don't use it to my advantage?" Then, the more rational part of me replied, "Are you a complete moron? You're thinking about jeopardizing your entire college career just to try to move from a B to an A in a Creative Writing class. Couldn't a creative person think of a better way to make that move?" Of course I could, but the crazy, adventurous side of me couldn't wait to get in there to look around.

So once again, after lunch, I headed over to the computer lab, found an isolated seat (plenty of which were available on a Friday afternoon), and logged in under Margaret's name. Did I just call her "Margaret?" Wow!

Sure enough, I got in easily. The tricky part, though, was finding the grades themselves. Most of the layout of the course was exactly the way students see things, and I started to worry that maybe the teachers had a separate system somewhere else. Determined to succeed and with plenty of time on my hands, I kept clicking on things until I noticed something called the "Control Panel," something that I had never seen on our student pages. And that's where all the extra teacher stuff was hidden. As I started clicking through that area, I realized I could set up new announcements or change the ones already posted. I could set up or alter Discussion Boards. I could even create quizzes if I wanted to. While that all sounded like a lot of fun and had the potential for some great pranks, I really wanted to see the grade book. So when I finally found it, I only hesitated for about two seconds before I entered.

There, of course, I saw not only my grades but the grades of all my classmates as well. No wonder some of them are pleading for help, I thought, and no wonder those girls are kissing up to Margaret. My grade of 89 was one of the highest averages in the class. She must be tougher than I thought. Or maybe all my classmates are really slackers. Only two people in the class – Betty and Willie – had averages over 90, and they are obviously brilliant. Those grades didn't surprise me at all. But everybody else was in the 75-to-85 range, and that really surprised me. Usually, at this school anyway, when most of the students are hovering between a C and a B, they're all complaining about how the teacher is too hard. Yet, even though most of the students are struggling a bit, I haven't heard anyone yet complain about Ms. Cavellari. She has obviously won over everyone with her sweet personality and her kind ways. Have I mentioned that she's also beautiful? I really couldn't believe what I was seeing.

I felt pretty good about my discovery, though, because I realized that I wouldn't have to tamper with my grades. If I were number three in the class with an 89 average, I might be able to still get an A even if I dropped a point or two. My history teacher told us at the beginning of the semester that most teachers are more than willing to bump a student up to a higher grade if the student has perfect attendance, does all the homework, and participates in class. Obviously, I'm doing all of that in this class, and I have the extra benefit of knowing that Ms. Cavellari is probably even nicer than "most teachers." I felt really good about my chances for an A after that view of the gradebook.

Something about having access to the gradebook, however, was still gnawing at me. Even though I didn't need to change any of my own grades,

I still wanted to know what it felt like to do so. So I scrolled up and down through the grades a bit more, trying to find something I could change, something that wouldn't really matter. That's when I noticed she had recorded the punctuation exercises we had done in the first few weeks.

She told us the grades on those exercises wouldn't really affect our final grade at all and that she was just trying to get a feel of where we were with our skills. But there they were. I had received an eight out of ten on commas, a six on semicolons, a seven on colons, a nine on apostrophes and hyphens, and a four on dashes. (I didn't have a clue about dashes. I had never used a dash in my life up to that point.). Overall, that was 34 out of 50 for a grade of 68, my lowest grade all semester – by far. (Notice the dash.)

So is it possible I had an average of 89 with a 68 thrown in? No, it was not. Just to make sure, I looked at all my other grades, and I figured out the average for myself. Just as she had said, Ms. Cavellari had not entered the grade from the punctuation exercise into our average for the course. That meant, if I wanted to, I could change one of my punctuation grades, and it wouldn't mean a thing. I could even lower one of those grades, and it wouldn't matter. So that's what I did. Can you believe that? I actually lowered the grade on the apostrophes-and-hyphens quiz from a nine to an eight, and I watched as the computer also changed the overall grade on those five quizzes from a 68 to a 66. I felt so cool.

Why would I lower a grade? I just had a crazy feeling that if somehow, someone suspected me of changing my grade, the fact that I lowered it would convince that person that I didn't do it. After all, why would anyone in his right mind lower a grade? He wouldn't of course. The other side of that reasoning, however, implies that since I did, in fact, lower my grade, I must not be in my right mind. Case closed.

Saturday, November 6

I love Saturdays. I always have. As a kid, I couldn't wait to get up on Saturday mornings to watch television, and now, as an adult (arguably anyway), I love sleeping in as long as I want. A bunch of us guys from the dorm went out last night to see that new movie called *The Social Network*, which is all about the beginnings of Facebook. The movie was really good, too. Then, afterwards, we went out for some food, and after that, we ended up playing a bunch of board games with some girls from the second floor. We played in the lounge area near the main entrance, and I didn't get to bed until about 4:00 a.m., so sleeping in was wonderful. I slept until noon, talked with Teddy for about a half hour before I pulled myself out of bed, and, then, I had to hustle over to the cafeteria to get something to eat before they closed at 1:00. I didn't even have time to shower.

We were talking about the movie at lunch, and I realized how little I actually know about Facebook. Yes, I have an account, and I even have a couple hundred "Friends," but I'm not on there that much, and I am nowhere close to being as addicted to it as some of my dormmates. And I get the feeling that some girls are even worse. I think the longest time I ever spent on Facebook was maybe a half hour – tops. These guys said they could easily spend two or three hours, jumping around from Friend to Friend, instant messaging everyone, and commenting on photos. Not me. I hate sending text messages – even on my phone. It takes way too long to carry on a conversation, and it's usually about stupid stuff that I wouldn't waste my time actually talking about unless I had to because I was killing time somewhere. I find, too, that as a writer, I'm a bit too anal. Even though nobody else cares, I don't want to make any spelling or punctuation mistakes, and I find that I'm always re-reading what I've written and making changes before I send it. As a result, if I'm instant messaging with someone, that person makes two or three comments for every one I make. I just can't keep up.

All that talk about Facebook, though, led me to – go ahead, and guess: yes, you're right – the one and only Ms. Margaret Cavellari. Why have I not yet looked her up on Facebook or Googled her for that matter? I do remember looking her up on "Rate My Professor," and, no surprise, everyone rated her as "Hot."

I was tempted to check her out right after lunch, but it was such a beautiful fall day, and the same crew from last night said they were going to play some touch football, so I postponed my computer surveillance and spent the afternoon doing my best Dustin Keller (tight end for the Jets) impersonation on the open field next to the science building. By my count, I scored six touchdowns. Of course, I probably gave up just as many on the defensive end. Who cares? We had a great time. It really felt awesome to be outside running around and having fun like a little kid again. I don't think I've had that much fun since the semester started. I better do more of that, or I might turn into a regular college geek.

Afterwards, I showered and ate, and since the college was hosting a fall festival in the Fieldhouse, I figured I'd head over there later to see what was going on. Before I did that, though, I went to Facebook and discovered that Ms. Cavellari apparently isn't a big fan of Facebook either. I found her page easily enough, but her Friends' list wasn't that much bigger than mine. I was a little surprised by that. Since I learned from the movie that the whole Facebook thing started in Boston, I guess I figured that she'd have thousands of Friends. And while there was a lot of activity on her page, I saw very few posts by her. Mostly, it was like her e-mail account: lots of stupid stuff. It looked like a lot of the people she went to high school and college with just kept posting the mindless activities of their days. Then, they would post even more mindless comments about other people's comments. I don't quite get it. And neither does Margaret apparently.

In fact, her few posts seemed somewhat similar to the stuff she said in class. She was always complimenting and encouraging others, but she rarely revealed anything about herself. One particular post did stand out, though: "I have this one cute, young student in my Creative Writing class named Tom Sullivan. He's adorable. He's about 5' 10" with curly blond hair, and he's a joy to have in class. He's always prepared and enthusiastic, and he always speaks up when no one else is willing to talk. I love him."

Okay, I admit, I made up that whole comment. But don't you think that's what she would write about me if she could? Yessss.

Naturally, I also checked her pictures while I was in there, and again, I didn't find much. The only thing that was really interesting was the collection of pictures that she has used over the years as her official Facebook photos. While some people have changed their image over a hundred times and have included some of the most ridiculous shots ever, she had used a grand total of eight pictures. The first one looked like it could have been from high school or first year of college because she looked so innocent and shy. Her hair was really short, she hardly looked at the camera, and her smile was a bit self-conscious. She probably didn't even know how beautiful she was; that's how innocent she looked.

In the next five or six shots, I could see her hair getting longer, and I could see her starting to come out of her shell. She looked at the camera with confidence, she laughed easily, and she even made a funny face in one photo. Then, she must have started applying for jobs because her last two were serious and professional. Now that she had a job, I figured she could change her picture again and show the relaxed and beautiful Margaret rather than the serious and beautiful Margaret. She's so much prettier when she smiles. Maybe I should text her that thought. I'm sure she'd love to hear from me. Maybe we could even become Friends. No, I couldn't do it. Oh, I could be her Friend if she requested me, but I couldn't ask to be her Friend. It would be too hard if she ignored me and even harder if she rejected me completely. I guess I'll have to save that idea for another day.

When I was about to Google her, the guys from the wing barged into the room and said, "We're going to the Fieldhouse." They didn't ask if I wanted to go to the Fieldhouse at that moment; they said, "We're going to the Fieldhouse." Feeling somewhat intimidated by the pressure and not wanting them to see whose face was on my computer screen, I quickly logged off and agreed to go with them.

When we got over there, the place was packed. They had all kinds of food booths with apple cider and apple-cider doughnuts, and they had a bunch of festival games set up as well. They also had a dunking booth, and the president of the college was sitting on the hot seat actually antagonizing the people in line to try and dunk him, and he was getting dumped into the water about every three minutes. It was hilarious.

Some of the games were mindless and fun like ring toss and darts, but some were extremely demanding and competitive. The National Guard had set up a huge chin-up bar, so lots of guys were showing off for the girls. And they also had two boxing rings where people could dress up in big Sumo wrestler suits and go at it, or else they could don headgear and use those big batons and beat each other up. As the original Wimpy Kid, I stayed far away from all that stuff, so I wouldn't get teased or pressured into participating. Fortunately, I succeeded.

When I saw Megan from our Creative Writing class working with another girl at the cotton-candy booth, they looked like they were being overwhelmed, so I offered to help out. "Oh, my God, yes," Megan said excitedly. "I've never seen so many people with such a strong desire for cotton candy. If you could just take tickets and keep this line in order, we could probably keep up without going crazy."

They really only needed me for about 20 minutes, and, then, the rush died down. Because I was having such a good time hanging out with Megan and her friend, Doreen, however, I stayed there the rest of the night. I had never seen Doreen on campus, and Megan explained that the two of them were roommates. Doreen is also an English major, so between the three of us – no, among the three of us – we had a great conversation about our courses and our teachers and our favorite writers. I was actually tempted to ask them what they thought of Mr. Masterson, but I was afraid the conversation wouldn't be as much fun, so I let it go.

When Megan and I told Doreen about our movie-making assignment, she was so jealous. "Oh, I would love to do that," she said. "In fact, if either one of you needs an actress to play a part for you, just let me know. I used to be in all the plays in high school, and I'd love to be in your stories." All of a sudden, I felt like a real movie director casting about for starlets, and I have to admit, I liked the feeling.

"You would really do that?" I asked.

"I would love to do that. Seriously."

Immediately, I began to plan how Doreen could be the star of my first movie.

Sunday, November 7

On Sunday, I slept late again, with an extra hour's sleep for the time change, but I did get up in time for the 11:00 church service on campus, and I made it to the cafeteria afterwards for lunch. By 12:30, I was ready for some football. The Jets were scheduled to play at Detroit, and I was ready too.

The serious student part of me wanted to get some work done, but the football crazy part of me wanted to watch the game. I always rationalize that the three hours that I spend watching the Jets each week is my down time. After all, everyone needs a little break from work. And Sunday is supposed to be a "day of rest," after all. The funny thing about the whole experience, though, is that I don't necessarily feel that great when the Jets win, but I feel totally miserable if they lose. After a loss, I feel like I just wasted three hours of my life, three hours I will never have back again. It's like I expect them to win, I want them to win, and they need me to be watching them to win, so if they lose, I lose too. I wonder if this behavior qualifies as an addiction. I want it, I can't go without it, yet, I'm never satisfied. I suppose if they win the Super Bowl this year, then I'll finally be satisfied. After all, they've never won the Super Bowl in my lifetime, not since 1969 when Joe Willie Namath guaranteed a victory and actually delivered a victory over the heavily favored Baltimore Colts.

So anyway, during the half hour before the game, I actually looked over my homework assignments for the week, and I laid out a few things that I might actually accomplish during the game's commercials, things like coming up with an idea for my video, beginning the Works Cited page for my history paper, and typing some words in this novel for November.

Who am I kidding? I do this every week, and I never get any work done during the game. I spend the commercial time getting refreshments or going to the bathroom. Or if Teddy is here or somebody else stops in to watch, I just talk about the game. Why can't I just forget about school for three hours and enjoy the game? I can. And I will. J – E – T – S. Jets. Jets. Jets.

Ten minutes before kickoff, though, I began thinking about school again. Sort of. I was thinking about Ms. Cavellari. Since I never got around to Googling her last night, I grabbed my laptop and began a quick search. I actually started with an image search because I thought that would be quicker and because I love looking at her. Amazingly, there were no other Margaret Cavellaris listed, and there were only three pictures of her posted on the web. One was her current Facebook picture, and the other two both looked like she had won some kind of an award in college. In one, she was shaking an older woman's hand, and in the other, she appeared to be receiving a check – for a scholarship most likely. I could have clicked on the links to get more details, but the game was about to begin, so I set my laptop aside and settled in to watch the Jets and the Lions.

The Jets pulled it out. Amazing. They played lousy the entire game, and they were playing the Lions for crying out loud. Granted, the Lions have improved the last few years, but they're still the Lions. The Jets fumbled five times in this game, and Mark Sanchez threw an interception as well. With four minutes left, we were down by ten points, 20 to 10. If I had any brains at all, I would have turned the TV off and done something else, anything else.

On top of that, most of the guys on this wing are Giants fans, and since they know I'm a big Jets fan, they kept popping in to give me a hard time. Fortunately, I am both stupid and stubborn. We scored a touchdown with about three minutes left to reduce the deficit to three, 20-17. Then, our defense held the Lions without a first down, they punted, and we got the ball back with about a minute and a half left. The first two plays looked terrible, but, finally, we hit a couple pass plays, the Lions committed a stupid penalty, and on the last play of the game, Nick Folk kicked a field goal to tie it. I was screaming like a fool, and, not surprisingly, no Giants fans were in sight.

After that, we won the toss, returned the kickoff, and with one long pass play from Sanchez to Santonio Holmes, we moved into field-goal position. It was a chip shot, and we escaped with a victory, improving to 6 and 2. On top of that, the Cleveland Browns played an amazing game and beat the New England Patriots, so the Patriots are also 6-2, but we have the advantage because we beat them earlier in the season. Amazing. Amazing. Amazing. I guess that's why I enjoy these games so much and don't even want to miss one play. Go Jets.

Then, after the game, I grabbed my computer to see how I did with my picks on the other games. In addition to competing online with my dad and my brothers, we have a pool here on the wing, and I've been doing pretty well there too. I'm in the top five out of about 20 guys. Today, though, I only picked four winners out of the first seven games. That's not so good. But I did pick the Patriots to win, so even though I lost that game in the pool, I'm okay with that because it helps the Jets in the standings. And maybe I can console Ms. Cavellari during class tomorrow. I probably shouldn't do that, though, because she never talks about football, and the only reason I know she's a Patriots fan is because I know her password.

So after checking the football pools, I went back to those two pictures of her I saw earlier, and I was right on both counts. She won a short-story contest when she was a junior in college, and at the end of her senior year, she won the English department award which entitled her to a scholarship for graduate study. No surprises there.

After that, I did a general search on her name in Google, and again, she was the only "Margaret Cavellari" listed. That must be a pretty unusual Italian name or an odd spelling, I thought, as I began searching down through the 11 listings for her name. Three of them linked back to the photos I had just seen, two went back to her days as a high-school swimmer, and the others linked to poems and short stories she had written. I was pretty impressed, I have to admit. I knew she was a published writer because she's always encouraging us to submit our stuff, and she even told us a story about a publisher who wanted to cut one of her short stories by about 30%. She said she told the editor that she was "unwilling to cut even one word." I'm sure I don't remember her exact words, but it was something like this: "I've worked on that particular story for over six years, and I feel pretty confident that the length is where it should be. If you are unable or unwilling to publish the story as is, I would rather submit it to another publication where it will live as a fully developed child rather than as one that is slightly deformed." I remember thinking that she must be tougher than she looks because she seems like such a soft touch, at least with us. In that situation, though, she really stuck up for herself, and she even used a metaphor in her response to that editor. That was pretty cool. And sure enough, she said the editor took the story without making a single change.

At the time, Ms. Cavellari was also trying to teach us that we don't have to automatically change our work just because somebody makes a suggestion. We have a lot of peer-review sessions in her class, and I think she thought we were all just blindly changing things just because one reader made a comment. I know I was. She reminded us that the work is ours, that we know exactly what we are trying to do, and that we should stand firm in our beliefs about our work even if we have to go against *her* suggestions.

"But won't that hurt our grade," one of the girls asked at the time, "if we go against what you tell us to do?"

"Not if you can explain yourself and justify the reason for what you're doing," she replied. Then, she went on to explain that creative writing is not at all like math where we're all going to have the same answer to a problem. She said she wants to see 24 different solutions to the problems she gives us. She is so cool.

She has already shown us in class one of her short stories and one of her poems, and, quite honestly, I didn't quite understand them the first time through. She uses a lot of symbolism, and she admits that she's writing primarily for women about women's issues, but she thinks men should be aware of the issues as well.

The poem was supposedly about how women still feel like they are on the fringes of society in some situations, and the story was about a long-time relationship that had gone bad. As she explained them to us, I wondered if she were writing autobiographically, but she never let on that that was the case. She admitted that she uses a lot of her personal experiences in her writing, but she also emphasized that she "tweaks" everything to make her points. In addition, she said that sometimes, she just imagines things entirely, and they have no connection whatsoever to her life or to reality.

Monday, November 8

Today is only the eighth day of November, and we already have our first heavy snowfall. I can't believe it. Nobody told me it was going to snow. It didn't even feel that cold this morning when I walked over to my first class, but as we were sitting in our Creative Writing class, the wet flakes started falling. And Ms. Cavellari was so cute. She made us stop what we were working on – a discussion of personification – so we could write a poem about the first snowfall of the season.

Then, she had us turn off our computer monitors, so we couldn't see what we were writing. She makes us do that periodically, so we don't edit our work too soon. She just wants us to go straight from our brain to the computer without stopping to think. At first, it was hard to do, but we've done this particular exercise so many times now that it's no big deal.

So I began writing about my paper route when I was 12 or 13 years old. That was the first thing that popped into my head. I can vividly remember delivering *The Daily Star* on Union Street. I remember one particular day when the snow was coming down like crazy, the wind was blowing, and I had to toss a paper up to the toughest porch on the route. This porch was on the third floor of this house, and the opening from the street was only about four feet wide and maybe six feet high. This was a tough shot even on good days. I knew if I missed, the paper would get soaked, so I took my time and tried to actually measure the speed and the direction of the wind. I felt like a field-goal kicker with the game on the line. Then, I tossed it as hard as I could about two feet to the left of the porch, and, sure enough, the wind brought it back, and the paper landed on the porch on the first try. That was my best toss ever. Looking back, I'm pretty sure that wasn't a first-snowfall story, but who cares? As Ms. Cavellari herself would say, I "tweaked" it to make a point.

And the actual poem? Fortunately, we didn't have to finish the poem in class. We just had to get some thoughts down on paper, and we have to bring the finished poem to class on Wednesday. So I have about a page and a half of notes, and I'm sure I can write a short poem about that experience.

Then, on the way to the cafeteria for lunch, a great thing happened: a snowball fight. I was just moving through the walkways near the dorms with Megan and Doreen, and we were about 100 yards from the cafeteria when the onslaught started. Five or six guys from Plassman Hall started firing snowballs at us. The girls took off and ran to the cafeteria, but I had handed my books to Megan, and I started firing back. Though we didn't have much snow on the ground, it was perfect packing for snowballs. Fortunately, there were two other groups from our class walking behind us, and they joined in too. Within minutes, it was all-out war. Guys came piling out of the cafeteria and the dorms, and we had all taken sides. Most of the walkers and the cafeteria guys were on one side of the walkway, and most of the dorm guys were on the other. A few girls got into it as well. I felt like I was home again for the first heavy snowfall. The best part, though, was still to come.

After about five minutes of us blistering the dorm guys, a whole bunch of them actually retreated into Plassman Hall. We were going crazy, like we just won the Super Bowl or something. We were yelling and screaming at them and still throwing a few snowballs at the few guys who were still out there, hiding behind trees. We should have gone in to eat lunch at that point, but we were all so pumped up that we just kept talking about how we had destroyed them. Then, it happened.

We saw some guy up on the fourth floor of Plassman Hall open a window, and he started playing the "Charge!" song on his trumpet, just like they do in the old movies. And while we were looking up at him, all the guys who had retreated into Plassman Hall circled around behind us and attacked us again. It was awesome. We battled back and forth for another 20 minutes or so before we actually ran out of snow. Besides, we were all soaking wet too. Finally, we headed into the cafeteria to eat.

Megan and Doreen ran up to me when I entered, and they were both so excited. "We watched the whole thing from the front window while we ate. You guys were great," Doreen laughed.

Then, Megan added, "I just wish we had one of those Flip cameras. That would have been so great to get that on film."

Though they were already finished eating, they both hung around while I ate, and we talked about our upcoming video projects. Megan thought she wanted to do some kind of a boyfriend-girlfriend drama, and I told them I was still undecided. In fact, I told them I didn't have any ideas yet. Actually, I lied. I was toying with the idea of having a student discover his teacher's password, but I still wasn't ready to reveal that secret to anyone.

When I got back to the dorm, I took a hot shower to warm up, and then I settled in with my laptop. After I checked my e-mail, I logged in to Margaret's account to see if she had responded to Mr. Masterson's invitation to the river cruise. Naturally, I had to scroll though a bunch of other stuff first, but I finally found her response, and, unfortunately, she said "Yes."

"Tony, that's so nice of you," she wrote, and, "Yes, I would like to go. We'll talk later in the week to figure out the details."

I couldn't believe it. And it didn't surprise me at all. It didn't surprise me because she's always so nice to everyone. She probably couldn't say "No" to him even if she wanted to. Yet, why couldn't she say she would drive there by herself and meet him there? Or why couldn't she say she was already planning on attending with some of the other women in the English department? What am I going to do with that girl?

While I was in her "Sent" e-mail folder, I also noticed that she had forwarded a few of her school e-mails to another e-mail account that she had with Yahoo. Her username there was pretty similar to her college e-mail, but, naturally, the extension was different: m-cavellari@yahoo.com. The messages looked like they were mostly notes to editors about her writing, so I got the feeling that she was trying to separate her writing e-mails from her school e-mails. The content of those e-mails was pretty boring – publication dates and editorial stuff – but I had a brilliant thought while I read them: What if she uses the same password for her personal e-mail? Is that possible? Would that be great or what?

Immediately, I jumped over to Yahoo.com to test my theory, and the brilliant one was right again. She must have had over a thousand e-mails in there, and they went all the way back to 2003. I'd probably be able to write her biography by the time I got through reading all of them. No, I wasn't really going to actually read all of them. That was a figure of speech. In fact, I didn't read any of them today because I had some other work that had to be done.

So as I left her account to begin work on my history paper, I felt a little bit like the kid who has cookies hidden away in his bedroom closet. He doesn't have to eat them all at once, but he can sneak back in there any time he's hungry. What a treat.

I decided to write my history paper on the assassination of President Kennedy. Everybody in my parents' generation talks about that day like it was yesterday. They remember every single detail, pretty much like the way everybody in our generation remembers 9-11. The only things I really know about Kennedy are that he started the Peace Corps, he pledged to put a man on the moon, and he supposedly dated Marilyn Monroe. Boy, she must have been something. Not only did she go with him, but she also married Joe DiMaggio, the old centerfielder for the New York Yankees, and Arthur Miller, the guy who wrote *Death of a Salesman* and *All My Sons*, two of my favorite plays. Funny thing, though, she doesn't do that much for me. I have never really cared for blondes. I have always preferred the dark Italian types, like Mrs. C.

Mrs. C. That's funny. That's what Fonzie always called Richie Cunningham's mother on *Happy Days*. That used to be one of my favorite shows when I was a kid. I always thought that I would have fit in well during the 1950's. I really like the whole soda-shop thing and the letter sweaters. I like that time period so much that I even own the DVD of *American Graffiti*. What a great movie. The whole story takes place in one night. How cool is that!

Speaking of movies, Denzel Washington has a new one coming out this week that I can't wait to see. I don't remember the exact title, but it's about a runaway train that he has to stop somehow. We saw the preview last week in the theater, and the same preview was on TV about eight times yesterday during the game. I definitely want to see that film on the big screen. A lot of guys don't want to pay full price for a movie, but I don't mind. After all, now that I'm going to be a movie maker myself, I have to support my fellow professionals.

Tuesday, November 9

Today was a bit warmer, and all of the snow had melted, so we were back to fall weather again. I was sitting in science class this morning, and it was pretty boring, so I took out my laptop and started taking notes, so I wouldn't fall asleep. The class was so boring, though, that even typing the teacher's comments was boring, so I switched over to Margaret's personal e-mails in her Yahoo account and began reading. A lot of it was plain, everyday stuff like making plans for the weekend, getting together with family once in a while, and news about old classmates getting new jobs or promotions. The one character who really stood out, though, was a guy named Ricardo, and one of his recent e-mails just begged me to read it.

The subject line said "We have to talk." When I read the message, though, I had to laugh:

"I miss you terrible. I know we can work things out. Please come back to Boston soon for a weekend, or plese tell me that I can come to se you."

How could she even correspond with a guy who can't spell "please"? I know everybody makes mistakes when they send e-mails, but she's an English teacher, for crying out loud. Why not take the time to impress her with your writing ability? I know I would if I were writing to her.

The guy's e-mail address was "Ricardo47@gmail.com," so that didn't tell me much about him. I guess I expected her to be corresponding with other teachers who had "edu" in their e-mail addresses. As I was thinking about this Ricardo guy, I was tempted to respond to him and invite him to the river cruise for this Saturday. Wouldn't that be funny? Mr. Masterson would have to deal with the old boyfriend. I guess that wouldn't be that funny for Margaret, though.

So anyway, I kept looking for other e-mails from Ricardo, and I discovered that misspelling words was something he did all the time, and his messages also seemed to have an edge about them, like he was always a bit annoyed with her:

"Forget about what I said in the past. Dam, that was just dum."

"I like your family, but do we have to spend soo much time with them. Give me a brake."

"Why cant you come home this wekend?"

Her replies to his comments and questions were pretty much what I expected: a mix of the too-sweet teacher and the firm-but-honest editor:

"I forgive you for what you said. However, I will not tolerate that kind of language."

"You know how important my family is to me, especially my dad, and with his health condition, I don't want to miss out on any time I can enjoy with him."

"Ricardo, I really think we need a time-out after all these years; not a break-up per se but a sabbatical of sorts to see how we feel and find out where we are as a couple."

Naturally, I expected a reply from him that asked "What's a sabbatical?" but I didn't see one.

Our science class was just about over, so I prepared to log off when I saw one more e-mail that caught my eye. This one wasn't from Ricardo but from a girl named Susie, and the subject line said "Reunion: Check out Classmates for details."

I was familiar with the Classmates web site because my mom had used it to organize the 30th reunion for her high-school class, so I knew that would be the next web site I checked for more information about Ms. Cavellari.

I was more hungry than curious, though, so I went to the cafeteria for lunch before I checked out that web site, and after lunch, I actually did some work on my snowfall poem before I continued my detective work.

That's actually my new method for school work. Whenever I'm tempted to do anything but school work, I always tell myself that I have to do a little work before I can reward myself with a fun activity. I came up with this strategy about a month ago because I was starting to fall behind in my work. I'd be tempted to read non-school stuff, like *Sports Illustrated* or a John Grisham novel, instead of my regular readings for class. So now, I have to work on my poem a little before I can go to that web site.

Here's what I have so far.

"Snowflakes falling.

Warm home calling.

But the newspapers must be delivered."

Is that pathetic or what? Ms. Cavellari always says our "first drafts will probably be terrible, but everything gets better from there." I sure hope so. I'm having a hard time matching the excitement of a first snowfall with the task of delivering 80 newspapers in the late afternoon when the sky is getting dark, and everyone else is settling in for supper. Maybe I should forget all the pretty, descriptive stuff and focus, instead, on the challenge of tossing that one newspaper to the third floor. I could pretend it's an athletic competition, and I'm battling against the elements like the Packers often do on the "frozen tundra" of Green Bay, Wisconsin. I'll have to give that idea some more thought and play with it a bit. I do think it has potential, though.

Okay, believe it or not, when I tried to get onto the Classmates web site with Ms. Cavellari's username and password, I couldn't get in. Unbelievable. Does she really have more than one password? That's amazing. I was starting to think that I could go almost anywhere with that password. And guess what else? I think I can.

After my first failure, I realized that maybe the password wasn't the problem. Maybe I needed to use her other e-mail address as her username instead of the college username. And sure enough, the combination of the Yahoo username and the college password let me in.

There, I discovered a bit more information about Ricardo and the information about her ten-year high-school reunion. The reunion is scheduled for Thanksgiving weekend, and some of her old buddies had posted notes for her.

"Maggie Girl, you better be there."

"Mags, don't miss out on the fun."

"Mi Cavellarita, yo te amo, and can't wait to see you."

Then, I began poking around even more in her Classmates' account, and I actually came across some pictures posted by one of her friends, and sure enough, there was Ricardo.

Someone named Jenny had set up an album of pictures from their five-year reunion, and I saw a group shot with Ms. Cavellari, Ricardo, and three other couples. He looked to be about 6' 2" and pretty well built, so he could easily kick the crap out of me if it ever came to that. He also looked like a fellow Italian-American, though with his disheveled look perhaps not as educated or as refined as Ms. Cavellari. And he must have been behaving at the reunion because she had her arm around his waist, and she had a big smile on her face. Of course, maybe she was just drunk. In any event, the picture was tagged with full names, and his full name was "Ricardo Almonte."

Since I didn't see anything else in there that seemed interesting, I switched over to Google to see what else I could learn about Ricardo. Unlike Ms. Cavellari's unusual name, his name alone generated quite a few hits, so I also checked "Images" in Google to make sure I had the right person. Unfortunately for Ms. Cavellari, Ricardo's image and name came up quite often in the pages of the Boston newspapers, generally in the crime reports.

Apparently, Ricardo had a history of ripping people off for home repairs, and, then, in some cases, becoming abusive and combative. From what I could tell, he spent some time in jail, he was now free, and he was trying to work his way back into Ms. Cavellari's life.

"Not on my watch," I thought, as if I were truly her defender and protector. Yet, what would I do if he showed up on campus? Challenge him to a game of Scrabble?

I could notify the security office on campus, I thought. Yeah, that would go over well. I could imagine the conversation.

"And what makes you think that this Ricardo guy would be a threat to Ms. Cavellari?"

"Well, I've been secretly reading her e-mails and . . . ."

I was stumped. I didn't know what to do. I had painted myself into a corner. I couldn't tell anybody what I knew, and I couldn't help her in any way. Frustrated, I logged off and went to work out in the gym.

I'm really not much of a workout guy, but sometimes I do find it helpful when I feel like I have to release some energy. And that's exactly how I felt at that moment. So as I worked my way around the circuit of weight machines, I set the weight higher than I normally do, and I tried to exhaust myself as quickly as I could. I also pretended, I have to admit, that I was building up my strength to take on Ricardo. Who am I kidding? He'd wipe the floor with me and leave me out to dry – whatever that means.

Later, while showering, I decided that since I couldn't beat Ricardo physically, I'd have to find another way of protecting my fair maiden from this evil monster. I even tried to think of stories I'd read or movies I'd seen where the skinny, little weakling gets the best of the strong man and wins the girl, but I must have been too exhausted because I couldn't think of a single thing. I knew there had to be examples out there, something like a modern-day David slaying Goliath with his slingshot. What could I possibly do to him? Everybody always says the pen is mightier than the sword, but no examples came to my mind. Like my first-snowfall poem, I guess I'll have to sleep on my ideas for a while and see if any good ones come to me.

Wednesday, November 10

When the time came for Wednesday's class, I couldn't wait to see Ms. Cavellari again. I had spent so much time reading about her or reading her e-mails that I was just eager to see her in person and listen to her speak. She really surprised me, though, because she was already there when I walked in.

"Oh, Tom, I'm so glad you're here. I really want to show this DVD to the class today, and the computer is not cooperating. Can you help me?"

"I'll give it a try," I responded with confidence – even though I wasn't 100% sure I could help her. So while I tried to play the DVD, she took attendance and distributed some worksheets.

"I'm pretty sure this computer is frozen; are you okay if I reboot it?" I asked when she returned to her desk.

"Sure, if you think that's all it needs."

"That's what I'm hoping."

"Alright, class, once you're logged in, go ahead and open a Word document. We're going to watch a short film today – assuming Tom can get my computer to work – and, then, we'll do a focused freewriting exercise."

While I was waiting for the computer to reboot, Ms. Cavellari walked around the classroom returning corrected essays and making small talk with everyone. She really has a nice way of making everyone feel comfortable, and she and a few of the girls were giggling over the image that Grace

Ferguson used as her screen saver: a full head shot of Yankee shortstop, Derek Jeter.

"He's got a girlfriend, ya know," I heard Ms. Cavellari say to Grace. "And besides, he's getting old."

"Yeah, but he just won another Gold Glove," another Yankee fan piped in.

I couldn't hear the girls' responses because another one of the guys interrupted and started giving Ms. Cavellari a hard time about being a Red Sox fan.

"Just because you went to school in Boston doesn't mean you have to root for those bums."

Meanwhile, the log-in screen finally popped up, and without thinking, I typed in Ms. Cavellari's username and password. At first, I wasn't aware of my error, but when her desktop screen popped up with her name up front, I realized my mistake, and I tried to think of a way to save myself.

"Are you ready for me to log in, Tom?" Ms. Cavellari asked as she returned to her desk at the front of the classroom.

"Almost," I lied. And I quickly hit "Control-Alt-Delete" to start the reboot process all over again. Then, I also turned off the monitor, so she couldn't tell what I was doing, and I pretended that the resolution settings were causing the problem. "Just let me adjust the monitor's display screen, so it doesn't impact the media download," I said finally, trying to use technical terms that might throw her off.

"Whatever you say, Tom," she responded, and she returned to speak to the class. Eventually, of course, the machine rebooted, and when the log-in screen appeared again, I asked her to sign in. Fortunately, despite my nervousness, I was able to get the DVD to play, and the rest of the class proceeded smoothly. What a hambone, I thought, as I settled comfortably back into my seat, a bit tense and a bit relieved at the same time.

The DVD she showed us was all about the writing process. Apparently, some English teachers at Harvard – Ms. Cavellari's alma mater – had tracked a group of about 400 students as they progressed through their four years of college. These teachers focused primarily on the writing assignments these students completed, not just for English but for all their subjects. Then, at the end, the teachers interviewed some of the students, and they all talked about what writing had meant to them during those four years and how they themselves had changed or progressed as writers. They also interviewed some of the teachers to get their thoughts on what they were trying to impress upon the students.

As I write that description, I realize that it sounds deadly boring, but the video was actually quite interesting. They had a nice mix of students (maybe seven or eight), and they all had different stories to tell. A lot of them admitted that they felt overwhelmed or intimidated at the beginning, but by the end, when we saw them, they all appeared confident and successful. One guy described a major paper that he worked on and how difficult it was for him, but he persevered and finished. One girl mentioned that English was her second language, so writing in English was especially hard for her, but she, too, fought through it and succeeded. And as they looked back at what they learned, they were all saying the same things that Ms. Cavellari and other English teachers say all the time about writing (get your thoughts on paper, get feedback, revise, revise, revise, etc.), but because these were kids our age speaking, I think it was easier to accept what they said and take it seriously. And maybe the fact that these were Ivy League kids added a little extra emphasis. For some reason, I assumed that all Ivy Leaguers are just naturally brilliant, and everything is a breeze for them. Who knew that they have doubts and uncertainties too? After we watched the video and wrote about it in our journals, we had a good discussion about it, and, then, Ms. Cavellari showed us another video; this one was from YouTube.

Since tomorrow is Veterans' Day, she wanted us to think about what our American soldiers have done for us, and, naturally, she wanted us to write about it, too, in our journals. And this video was amazing. The video is called "Requiem," and I was the only one in the class who knew that a requiem is a funeral song. (I think Ms. Cavellari was impressed that I knew that; my Catholic upbringing helped me out again.) So anyway, she explained that a friend of hers is from Amsterdam, New York, which is only about 30 miles west of here, and this friend showed her this video. The song is about all the soldiers from Amsterdam who died during World War II, and there were about 150, which is quite a few from such a small town.

The song describes the different ethnic backgrounds and experiences of all these soldiers, and the narrator mentions their going-away parties. Then, it describes the various war settings and the way the soldiers died, and it ends with the idea that they died for the people of their home town. Just the song alone is pretty touching.

But in addition to the music, the video shows the pictures of all these men. Most of them are in their military uniforms, and underneath the pictures are their names, their dates of death, and where they died. It's really amazing to see all these young faces and to imagine what it must have been like for their families to have to deal with their deaths and to bury them. Afterwards, too, somebody mentioned that it must have been quite a loss for that town to lose so many of its young men over a four- or five-year period. The whole thing was really powerful, and it gave me a much better appreciation of what these young men gave up for the rest of us, and it made me think about the guys that I know who are now in the military. Quite honestly, I don't have a strong desire to enlist, but after seeing this video, I feel like I would be willing to go if they really needed me like they did during World War II. In fact, afterwards, Ms. Cavellari asked if there were any veterans in the class, and we actually have two – one male and one female – and I never would have guessed either one of them was a soldier. The girl is currently in the National Guard, and the guy served a year and a half in Iraq. Both of them are so quiet and unassuming; the class actually gave them a round of applause after they identified themselves and briefly described their service.

What a great class, and what a great bunch of people in this class. I feel like we're really bonding as a group, and I think it has a lot to do with Ms. Cavellari. She is so great at exposing us to different things, then making us write about them, and getting people to open up and talk about what they've written. She has one quote that she uses all the time to get us to write, and it's something like "how can I know what I'm thinking unless I write it down?" She told us who said it, but I don't remember, and anyway, I find that our class discussions are so much better after we've written about the subject for a few minutes. Some people are eager to share what they've written, and, then, other people either respond to those thoughts, or they share similar or dissimilar ideas. Then, near the end of class, someone mentioned that the Student Senate was hosting a free pizza party in the Student Union at noon and that we should all go there for lunch, and most of us did. Even Ms. Cavellari. It was awesome. We put three tables together, and we just enjoyed one another's company. I've never seen that happen before with any of my classes. Some kids even left late for their 1:00 classes because they lost track of time.

I can't believe I wrote almost 1,700 words (my daily quota) on just that one class. I've never done that before, but it's pretty quiet in the computer lab tonight, so maybe that had something to do with it. I expected this place to be a lot busier with kids working on term papers and stuff, but, apparently, everybody's waiting until the last minute, just like I've done with this first-snowfall poem. Fortunately, Ms. Cavellari forgot to collect our poems today, so I have a little extra time now – until Friday, at least.

So what have I got? Nothing. Still stuck. I'll be back later with something, I'm sure.

Thursday, November 11

So today is actually Veterans' Day, and guess what? I have to go to class after I finish working this shift at 8:00 a.m. What happened to honoring our soldiers by taking a day off from school? That's what we did in high school. When I asked one of the upperclassmen, he said it had to do with the three-hour evening classes that meet only once a week. Apparently, they make the schedule out, so that each day of the week gets one day off during the semester. So, since we have Thursday the 25th off for Thanksgiving, they couldn't also give us this Thursday off for Veterans' Day. I didn't quite understand when he explained it to me, but, then, he made it clearer. "Look, you idiot. (I hate it when people talk to me like that, but it does make me pay attention.) If your class meets three times a week, missing one of those classes on a Thursday is no big deal, but if your class meets only once a week on Thursday night, then it's like you miss three classes instead of one, and they can't do that because then you won't have enough class hours to qualify for three credit hours."

Okay, I get it now. Does that mean I'm not an idiot any longer? I doubt it, at least not in his eyes.

Actually, most of the upperclassmen have been pretty friendly here. I thought they might give me a hard time because I'm new and all, but they treat the transfer students better than they do the freshmen. During our first week on campus, the guys on our floor had a big get-together, and they made each of the freshmen sing their high-school alma maters, just like they do in some of the football training camps in the NFL. Since there were three transfer students on the floor, they made us be the judges, so it was like an *American Idol* show. I didn't have the heart to be as harsh as Simon Cowell, so I was more like Randy, and I kept saying "Yo, Dawg." The upperclassmen loved it. In fact, some of them still call me "Randy" as a result.

And believe it or not, they even have a few fraternities here on campus. I thought those things died out in the 1950's, but I guess these fraternities are different from the old days. If you want to join, you don't have to go through any hazing or anything; you just have to sign up and agree to be part of a cooperative housing venture. Apparently, it's cheaper than living in the regular dorms, but you have to be willing to cook for everybody once in a while, you have to do a certain number of chores each month, and you have to actually be in good academic standing to get admitted in the first place. Then, you have to maintain your grades, or you could be asked to leave the frat house. I couldn't believe it when it was described to me. What ever happened to *Animal House*? Am I thinking about joining for next semester or next year? I don't think so. Maybe if I came in as a freshman, I might, but I'll only be here for two years, and, as I mentioned before, I really like the dorm life the way it is. I might even consider becoming a resident assistant because they cut your housing cost in half, and the job doesn't look to be that hard.

Alright, let me give this first-snowfall poem one more try:

Saturday morning.
My friends sleep in.
I am up and out and sliding down Glen Avenue.
The first snow has fallen during the night
and continues to come.
Ten inches and growing.
My boots make the first footprints in the street.
The parallel snowbanks show that the plow must have come
through earlier,
but no tire tracks are visible now.
I see the lights in kitchens and the glow of television cartoons.
The only sound I hear is my breath exhaling,
and I watch the smoke escape from my lips.
I must collect the weekly charge for the newspaper.
I must knock on the doors and ring the bells.
Two-fifty a week with a fifty-cent tip if I'm lucky.
Only Harry DeVoe will give me a five-dollar bill and say, "Keep
the change."
I will never forget Harry DeVoe.

Friday, November 12

I read my new poem over this morning, and I actually like it. One draft too. I toyed with the idea of throwing the newspaper to the third floor against the wind, but I didn't care for it. I even considered the busyness of a late afternoon when people are out cleaning off their cars and shoveling the sidewalks, but I didn't care for that either. I always picture the first snowfall late at night or early in the morning when no one is outside. The snowfall I'm picturing here is not the heavy, wet snow that is good for snowballs but the light and fluffy snow that is just really pretty. I realize the pretty snow doesn't always fall late at night or early in the morning, but that's the way I picture it, and that's the way I like it. For me, the first snowfall should be quiet, almost reverential, like a church. Watching the snowfall is like watching God create in the Garden of Eden. I have often been shoveling our long driveway late at night and stopped to lean on my shovel and watch God's tender mercies drift down upon us. The moment is so peaceful, so serene. That's my picture of a first snowfall.

Wow! Where'd that come from? Some of that is really good, and maybe I'll change my poem entirely. I must have dreamed some of it without realizing it because when I woke up this morning, I had a good feeling about the poem, but it was more like a funny feeling because the original poem had a humorous twist. After all the narrator says about the beauty of the morning, he concludes that what he really remembers is the one guy who gave him the biggest tip. I guess that's more of a commercial take on a big Christmas tip than a spiritual recollection of a beautiful moment. And, in fact, Harry DeVoe tipped big every week, not just on Christmas which, of course, made him so memorable.

So maybe if I have time, I will revise my second version of the snowfall and use that in class, instead. Or maybe I'll just tell Ms. Cavellari about both versions and see what she has to say. She has spoken to us in the past about the importance of incubation, of letting our ideas sit for a while before we try to revise them. She says that our unconscious minds work on what we've written even while we are doing other things. Ideally, she wants us to have our first drafts done at least a day in advance, so we can sleep on them, and I guess that's what I did here. Now, my feeling about the first snowfall is more serious without the comical ending. Maybe I should combine the two in some way.

On the way to Ms. Cavellari's class, I saw Megan and Doreen walking up ahead of me, so I ran to catch up to them. I've also found myself thinking about Doreen quite a bit, and I haven't done anything about it. She was on her way to her science class, and the three of us got talking about the weekend ahead. "We should do something together," I blurted out without really thinking it through. I don't think I would have had the courage to just ask out Doreen at this point, but turning the "date" into a small-group activity with our mutual friend, Megan, makes it safe and easy. And I'm good at safe and easy.

"You know what we should do?" Megan said almost immediately. "We should go on one of those river cruises on the Hudson. Everyone says they're a blast."

Are you kidding me? I thought, as the idea sank into my skull. She didn't really just say that, did she? Yes, she did. Was that a good idea? I wondered. Or was that a bad idea? What should my reaction be here? I can't tell them why I think it might be a bad idea because I'm not supposed to know about the faculty get-together; I read about it in Ms. Cavellari's e-mail after all.

Fortunately, my temporary uncertainty was quickly overcome by my natural desire to please others (which I diagnosed during my psychology class last year), and I responded positively. "Yes," I said with a big smile, and I increased my enthusiasm with the thought of going to this event with Doreen. In fact, I think I even turned up my enthusiasm a notch, so I wouldn't have to show my hand so early in the game. Yes, I was definitely interested in her, but she didn't need to know that just yet because I didn't really know her that well. Yes, she was adorable in a cute kind of way, but some girls have a way of becoming annoying quickly, and I didn't want to commit to her if I didn't have a bigger sample of evidence. (Another academic phrase from somewhere.) "We should definitely do that," I added.

"What about you, Doreen? Are you in?" Megan asked.

"How much does it cost?" She asked shyly.

Since I didn't know the price and since she seemed to be asking Megan, I waited quietly, but I knew that asking the price was a buying sign, a sign of definite interest. (Business class, no doubt. Who knew I was actually learning so much?)

"Don't even worry about the money. Tom and I have you covered: don't we, Tom?"

"Of course we do." I answered. Then, to put Doreen at ease, I added. "Of course that means you'll definitely have to be in my movie now."

"Oh, I can't wait. Have you actually done any work on it yet?"

Just like that, the conversation shifted, which was fine because we had just entered Dugan Hall, and we had to separate to go to our classes. "Not much," I told her, "but we'll talk soon."

"Yeah," Megan jumped in. "Tom and I will get all the details about the cruise, and we'll get back to you. See you later."

I was flying. I was psyched. I was pumped.

I was also a bit nervous.

"Good morning," Ms. Cavellari said as we all settled in at our computer desks around the perimeter of the room. "Go ahead and open your computer journals and write for a few minutes while I take attendance and post the homework for next week."

"You start writing," Megan whispered to me, "and I'll go online to find out about this cruise. But don't let Margaret see me. Cover for me, or distract her if you have to."

I laughed. We were in the corner off to Ms. Cavellari's right, so she probably wouldn't even look that way. (Most teachers look forward toward the "action zone" of the classroom; I got that from a study-skills course.) But even if she did catch Megan surfing the net for cruise tickets, what's the worst that could happen? Since Megan never does that stuff, Ms. Cavellari would probably ignore it or make a joke out of it. We have one gamer in the class, Arthur, and he's always playing when he should be writing, but Ms. Cavellari just teases him. "What time is your Gamers Anonymous meeting?" she might say, or she'd sneak up behind him and turn off his monitor, which really freaks him out because he thinks he's lost his game without properly logging out. Fortunately, he's got a good sense of humor about it too. If he were really addicted, like some of the guys I see in the dorms or the computer labs, I'd be worried.

So anyway, I was psyched about the chance to spend time with Doreen, but a little part of me was nervous because Ms. Cavellari might see me with Doreen. Big deal, you might think. But the really optimistic and foolish dreamer part of me is still holding on to the possibility that Margaret and I might hit it off some day. Crazy thought, I know. But why not dream big?

"It's only twenty bucks a person," Megan whispered, "but get this; they have an online special right here for Saturday night. All we have to do is print three coupons, and we can each get in for ten. That's so cool. I'll print the coupons later."

At that point, I stopped writing in my journal and switched over and opened up my snowfall poems. I quickly edited my second version down to the following:

Our driveway is long.
The snow is deep and still falling.
I shovel, alone in the dark
With the moon and the stars as my supervisors.

Back and forth I walk: one trip empty, one trip full.
The narrow drive is like a church aisle –
So serene and so peaceful –
and I clear the way for fellow believers.

Hot and tired, I remove my jacket and hang it on a tree.
Then, I lean against my shovel and watch,
As if in the Garden of Eden,
God drops his tender mercies upon us.

"Oh my God, Tom Sullivan! That is so beautiful."

Margaret had scared the daylights out of me. She had snuck up behind me and was watching me edit. She does that a lot, but usually she warns us that she'll be walking around observing, and usually it doesn't bother me. This time, though, because I was so engrossed in my changes, I didn't realize she was there, and my fellow conspirator, Megan, didn't cover for me at all. Nice.

"Please print a copy right now, right this second."

I did as she told me, and she walked up to the teacher console and switched from her computer screen to the overhead feature. Then, she took my poem and placed it on the glass, so everyone could see it displayed on the screen behind her.

"May I read it, Tom?" She asked.

"Sure," I said, embarrassed and honored at the same time by all the attention. Typically, she makes us read our own stuff, but she was really psyched about this one. And she read it with just the right feeling and with all the pauses in the right spots. Maybe we were actually more connected than even I imagined.

"First, tell us where this poem came from, Tom."

So I mentioned my first few miserable attempts, and then, I described the one about Saturday morning, collecting from the customers on my paper route. Finally, I explained how I felt differently about my original poem the following morning and how I had just revised what was a paragraph into a poem.

"Isn't the writing process so amazing?" She added. "Sometimes, you really don't know where you're going, but if you just keep typing or writing, the words and the ideas come out of you in new ways and better ways. I love this poem, Tom. I love it. What do the rest of you think?"

A couple classmates commented on the personification in line four and the simile in line six, and, I have to admit, I was pleased that they recognized these literary techniques. I actually felt like a real poet as they discussed my work.

"Where'd you get that line about the 'tender mercies'?" Arthur asked. "I like that."

"I saw an old Robert Duvall movie with that title once, and I'm pretty sure the phrase is from the Bible, though I couldn't tell you where."

Margaret jumped in at that point: "And that line about the Garden of Eden?"

I'm pretty sure she knew what I was trying to do, so I think she just wanted to hear me explain it to the others. "Well, because we had been talking previously about the 'first snowfall' of the season, I was playing with the idea of the first snowfall ever, as if God were creating it at that moment and showering it down upon us as just another wonderful and beautiful gift."

"Tom," Margaret continued. "You have to submit this poem to the College's literary magazine."

"Yeah," Megan added, "and maybe you could take a snowfall picture this winter to accompany the poem."

"That's a great idea," Margaret spoke again. "Oh my God, this class is really cooking now. Who else has a great poem that we can put up here on the overhead?"

The rest of the class flew by. We probably discussed three or four more poems, and people were really getting into it. I had never seen another class so excited about writing before. And before she dismissed us, Margaret reminded us again about the possibility of making movies for our final project. "I think we're really going to see some great works come out of this class."

Personally, I couldn't even think about my movie yet; I was still too excited and amped up about the positive reaction to my poem, especially Ms. Cavellari's reaction.

Megan printed the coupons for the cruise, and the two of us walked toward the cafeteria for lunch. "Should we wait for Doreen?" I asked.

"No, I think she said she has something else to do today. You like her, though, don't you?"

I hesitated. By the look on Megan's face, however, I could tell she knew. "Is it that obvious?"

"Actually, it isn't. I don't think most people would notice, and I don't think Doreen knows yet, but I have a gift of discernment about these things."

"A gift of discernment?"

"Yeah. I just know. I can see these things before anybody else can."

"Really?"

"Really."

"I can tell that you like Ms. Cavellari too."

"Who doesn't like Ms. Cavellari?"

"Yeah, but you really like her, more than most."

"Is that obvious to everyone else?"

"No, I don't think so. But I watch. I observe. Most people are so caught up in their own stuff that they don't see what other people are doing. Me – I'm different. I'm going to be a psychologist, so I spend a lot of my time just watching people, to see what they're up to."

"So you're watching everybody, not just me."

"Don't get a big head, Mr. Robert Frost."

"So what else do you see?"

"I see that you want to know if I watch Doreen and if she's at all interested in you."

"And?"

"And she is, but she doesn't know it yet."

"Really! How do you know that?"

"What? That she likes you or that she doesn't yet know that she likes you."

"Both." We were standing outside the cafeteria now.

"I just know."

"You just know; what kind of scientific answer is that?"

"That's all you're going to get today, my child. C'mon let's eat."

After lunch, I went back to the dorm and took a nap. I do that a lot on Friday afternoons. There's something about working that midnight to 8:00 a.m. shift on Wednesday night into Thursday morning that throws me off, and on Friday afternoon, I find it easy to doze off.

I woke up about three hours later and sat down with my laptop to make my NFL picks for the weekend. When I logged in, I realized that I missed out on Thursday's game between the Ravens and the Falcons. I'm usually on top of that stuff, so I was bummed out for a while before I noticed that the Falcons won. I wasn't planning to pick them, so I would have gotten that game wrong anyway.

After I made my picks, I checked my e-mail, and Megan had sent me one that said we had to be down at the dock by 7:00 p.m., tomorrow night in order to take advantage of the coupons. She also reminded me that I had offered to drive, so she and Doreen would meet me near the front of the library at 6:30.

After that, I checked on Ms. Cavellari's school e-mail to see if she were still going to the cruise with Mr. Masterson, and he had given her a similar message.

"Margaret,
I'll swing by and pick you up about 6:30, so we can go on that river cruise. I'm really looking forward to it, and I hope you are too.
Tony"

I found myself feeling a bit jealous even though I still didn't feel she would ever be interested in him.

Then, I noticed something unusual. The next e-mail was from Ricardo. He was still begging to see her, but the unusual part was that he sent his e-mail to her school account. Previously, I had only seen his e-mails come through her Yahoo account. Somehow, he must have found out where she was teaching, and he had somebody help him find her Kennedy College account. Okay, maybe he figured it out on his own, but I didn't see him as being that computer literate.

In any event, I next did something spontaneous and stupid. I clicked back on Tony's e-mail with the string of prior messages about the cruise included, and I quickly forwarded it to Ricardo at his e-mail address. I'm not sure exactly why I did that, but a few thoughts came to mind.

One part of me was mad at Ms. Cavellari for agreeing to go with Tony Masterson in the first place. Idiotic, I know. Another part of me wanted her to be done with this stupid Ricardo once and for all, and I was hoping he would get the hint once he received the forwarded e-mail. But obviously, I wasn't thinking clearly. For some reason, I felt like I was sending Ricardo an anonymous message to let him know that Margaret wasn't interested in him. I felt like the situation would be okay because Ricardo would have no idea who t-sullivan@kennedy.edu was.

Then, the stupidity of what I had done hit me. Since I was in Margaret's account and not my own when I forwarded the e-mail, it would look like she had sent it to Ricardo as a way of breaking up with him forever. And Ricardo, even as dumb as I assumed him to be, would see that the e-mail came from her and react accordingly. I also realized this after the fact, but once Ricardo got that e-mail, he could do one of two things. He could take a hint and never bother her again. Or, he could be so upset by the way that she had notified him that he might actually show up at the dock at 6:30, just like everyone else. And that's exactly what he did.

Saturday, November 13

Saturday morning was gorgeous, so gorgeous in fact that I decided to drive home to visit my parents. They love it when I stop in unannounced, and I arrived just in time to help my dad rake up the remaining leaves and cart them off to the landfill. When we returned to the house, Mom had sandwiches, snacks, and lemonade waiting for us, and we sat out on the back deck and swapped stories about our week. They told me about the new floor they were going to put in the upstairs bathroom, and I told them about how well I did on my mid-term grades. Mom especially loved to hear that I was doing so well and enjoying college so much. I wanted to tell them about my poem and about the reception that it received, but I felt a little funny about it, probably because we never really talk about stuff like that in our home. We always talk about practical and safe subjects, like rain gutters and report cards, not God and the beauty of a snowfall. I also told them about the cruise later that night, and they both warned me to have fun but to stay sober. They said they heard a story about a young man who actually fell over the side of the boat and into the river during one of those cruises. I was a bit skeptical about that story, but Mom insisted that it was true because she heard it at the beauty parlor. Dad and I laughed when she said that, so she threw small pickles at both of us.

"I don't care if you don't believe me; just be careful, and if you do get drunk, make sure you have a designated driver."

"I'll behave, Mommy; I promise," I said like a five-year old, and she and Dad laughed at me this time.

Later, when I returned to campus and prepared to go on the cruise, I couldn't figure out what to wear. I know that sounds girlish, but the cruise thing was throwing me off. Since they have drinking and dancing on the boat, I didn't know if I should dress like I was going out to a club. Or, since they also have an outside deck where we can sit and just enjoy the ride, should I dress like I'm going on a picnic? And how cold does it get on the river at night anyway?

Eventually, I decided on a compromise outfit. I wore a nice pair of blue jeans, so I could still look okay and still sit on the outside deck if I wanted to. And I wore a nice shirt for the dance floor with a sweater and jacket over it just in case it got cold outside.

When I picked up the girls, they shared with me their own wardrobe dilemmas, and they also said a bunch of Kennedy students were going to attend, so we should have a good time. Megan was still teasing me about being Robert Frost, but I didn't care because then she had to explain the whole thing to Doreen, so Doreen got to learn what a sensitive guy I am. And girls love that stuff, right. I hope so; this girl anyway.

When we arrived at the river, we found free parking spots in the big garage nearby and headed up to the boat. Surprisingly, they had a photographer present to take pictures of everyone before they boarded, and the photographer explained that our picture would be available later that night when we returned if we wanted to purchase a copy. So I stood in the middle of the two girls, and they both put their arms in mine like I was escorting them down the aisle at a wedding. It was so sweet. I hope the picture looks good, so we have a nice souvenir of the evening.

Once we boarded the ship, we had to wait for everyone, so we just hung out on the upper deck and watched the others as they arrived. There was a bit of a breeze up there, but it was still a beautiful night with lots of stars in the sky. Naturally, I was looking out for Margaret and Tony, and they arrived with a whole bunch of teachers.

Megan tugged at my sleeve and said, "Hey, Tom, look who's here."

Again, I had to act surprised, so I also acted stupid. "Wow, who is that she's with?"

"That's Mr. Masterson, you idiot. I told you about him a while back."

"Oh, he's the guy you were talking about?"

While we were having that conversation, Doreen saw a bunch of her friends, so she started screaming to them: "Allie. Connie. Marisa. Look up. We're over here."

The whole boarding process took a long time, what with the

photographer and the big crowd. We didn't prepare to leave until almost 7:45. And just as they were about to pull up the walkway from the dock to the boat, I saw one last guy sprinting toward the boat from the parking garage. He didn't even have time to pose for a picture. You guessed it: it was Ricardo.

As the ship left the dock, most people stayed outside to look at the downtown city lights of Troy. Like everyone else, I was trying to identify various buildings as we passed them, but I was also keeping my eye on Ricardo to see what he was doing. Megan and Doreen and I were also watching the teachers, and we estimated that their group had about 50 people in it, but Megan and Doreen said only about 30 or 35 were Kennedy College faculty, and the rest were probably spouses or significant others. Naturally, a group that big didn't all stay together, and Ms. Cavellari and Tony seemed to be in a group of about eight or ten people, and the girls said most of them were English teachers.

I was pleased to see that Ms Cavellari and Tony weren't off in a corner by themselves. In fact, they weren't even talking to each other. Two other guys seemed to be hitting on her, though, while Tony spoke to another lady. Since their group was on the upper deck with us and pretty heavy in conversation, I don't think Ms. Cavellari had any idea that Ricardo was on board. That was good for the moment, but I knew that had to change. The boat wasn't that big, and Ricardo didn't come all the way from Boston to simply look at the Troy skyline.

As I watched him, I was a little relieved. He didn't look as big in person as he did in the pictures online, and he didn't seem to be as aggressive and macho as I made him out to be. Obviously, he was out of his element, but he seemed very tentative as he made his way up the stairs toward the second deck. Then, once he got up there, he remained in a corner near the rear of the boat, and he appeared to be scanning the crowd of people looking for his beloved.

"Tom, are you okay?" Doreen asked. "You seem like you're off in a faraway place."

"Oh, yeah. I'm sorry. I'm fine. Whenever I get on a river, I get somewhat mesmerized because I get to see familiar sights from a new perspective." (What a recovery.) "Look at that restaurant over there, for example. It's an Italian restaurant called Altieris, and our family has been there many times, but I've never seen it from this side. It looks so small and old from here, but it's huge inside and fully modern too."

"Hey, it feels like the boat is turning," Megan said. "Why is that?"

"I'm pretty sure we cruise south, down past Albany, because the Albany skyline is more attractive than heading north toward Waterford where there's not much to see."

"How do you know that?"

"I have a computer, too, you know."

"Really? And you know how to use it?"

"What's with you two?" Doreen asked. "You're like a brother and sister."

"Well, she resents the fact that I have to explain everything to her in Creative Writing class."

"There's a nice piece of fiction right there," Megan retorted. "Hey, let's go inside and get drinks. And we can check out the rest of this boat too."

So in we went, and I couldn't believe how big the boat was. I mean I had a general idea and all, but in the center of the main room, there was a wide staircase that led up to another level. The main floor had a bar at each end with tables all over the place, and there was a big dance floor near the staircase. The disc jockey was nearby and he was trying to get people to dance, but he wasn't having much luck. Everyone was just wandering around, and we did the same. I bought each of us a beer, and we headed upstairs.

The lights were dimmer up there, and the tables were smaller. It looked like that might be the place where people would go if they wanted a bit more privacy. Megan seemed to realize that immediately and said, "Let's go back down; there's nothing up here."

"Do you girls want to sit?" I asked when we got back downstairs, "Or just hang out?"

"We want to dance," said Doreen, and she grabbed our beers, set them on a table near where some of her friends were sitting, and dragged Megan and me out to the dance floor. Fortunately, another group of people felt the same way at that moment as the music got louder and the pace picked up. Within seconds, we were in the midst of a mob. The party had started.

I'm not much of a dancer, I have to admit, but I do like to jump around out there when the music is rocking, and the music was definitely rocking, though I couldn't name the artist or the song. It was just fun. We danced through about three or four songs when Megan said she needed a break, though I think she was really trying to help me out.

"She's a wimp," Doreen called out. "Don't leave me alone out here, Tom."

I looked over at Megan to see if she wanted me to sit down with her, and she quickly waved me off. Honestly, I don't think Doreen needed me either because she was now also singing along with an imaginary microphone in her hand, and she looked like a real rock star.

As I was admiring her, I saw somebody waving at me. It was Ms. Cavellari. She was standing off to the side with her group, and when I waved back and motioned for her to join us, she also waved me off and gave me a thumbs up, for my dancing prowess, no doubt. Seeing her reminded me that I hadn't yet seen Ricardo inside, so I began scanning the crowd just as he had done earlier. And sure enough, he had found another corner, up near the bar, and it looked like he was checking out Ms. Cavellari. No surprise there. He was still pretty far away from her, though, and in the dark, it was hard to make out people's faces.

The whole scene was somewhat surreal. I came with Megan and Doreen, so I felt a certain obligation to stay with them, but I also wanted to be alone with Doreen at some point, and I wanted to keep an eye on Ms. Cavellari and Tony Masterson, and I felt obligated to watch Ricardo, too, so he didn't do something stupid, all because I had a senile moment in front of my computer screen. And did I mention that in my most optimistic of fantasies, I was also hoping to dance with Ms. Cavellari before the night was over? I'm sure she wanted to talk more about our common interest in writing and about our similar sensitivities. What a dreamer! What a dreamer! What a dreamer!

After a few more songs, even rock star Doreen was starting to get tired, so we stopped dancing and joined Megan and her friends at their table. We were sitting for a while when I noticed Ricardo moving closer to the bar. I was a little nervous, but I decided to head over there, too, to try and get some kind of a feel of what to expect from him. I figured I was safe because he had no idea who I was, and if anyone were in the line of fire, it would have to be Tony Masterson, who was now on the dance floor with Ms. Cavellari.

Since Ricardo was alone near one end of the bar, I went and stood right next to him in the small space at the end, but I acted like I didn't even see him. When I ordered my beer, I stayed at the bar drinking just to see what would happen next. He was drinking his beer much more quickly than I, and he was still intensely watching the dance floor.

"This is a pretty cool boat, isn't it?" I said just to see if he would respond.

"Not bad. I seen better."

"Really, where?"

He gave me a look like he couldn't be bothered making small talk with a stupid college kid, but, finally, he grunted: "Boston's got a huge boat out in the harbor, and they could probably fit two of these boats inside."

"No way."

Again, he looked at me like I was a moron.

Then, just as he appeared to be ready to say something else, he froze. He was looking straight at the dance floor, and I began to freeze up myself. I had an idea of what was coming.

Sure enough, Ms. Cavellari and Tony Masterson were walking toward us. They were talking and laughing, and I don't think she saw either me or Ricardo. Tony approached the bar with Ms. Cavellari on his right, so that he stood between the two former lovers, and I was off to Ricardo's left.

"What would you like to drink, Margaret?" I heard Tony say.

"Red wine, please."

As he turned to order, Ms. Cavellari saw Ricardo.

"Ricardo? Is that you?"

"Hello, Margaret."

"What are you doing here?"

"You invited me; didn't you?"

Her face said she had no idea what he was talking about, and I felt so guilty. She looked both embarrassed and afraid.

"Is something wrong?" Tony asked when he realized something was going on.

"None of your business, pal."

"First of all, I'm not your pal, and, second, I think this is my business."

At that point, Ricardo pushed Tony away, and he fell to the floor.

Like a crazy man, I wrapped my right hand around Ricardo's neck and held him in a headlock like my brothers did to me all the time when I was little. I fully expected to be thrown to the floor myself at any moment, but three Kennedy College football players jumped in as well as two security guys from the boat.

"Easy, big fella," one of the Kennedy College guys said to me as they pulled my arm from Ricardo's neck, and, then, the security guys were escorting Ricardo to the other side of the room. Ms. Cavellari was helping Tony up from the floor, and when she realized I was in the middle of the action, too, she did another double take.

"Tom? Are you okay?"

"I'm fine." I was lying, of course. I knew I had no chance whatsoever against the Boston Brawler, but I felt like I had to do something since it was all my fault. I think I was still shaking a bit when Doreen also rushed up to check on my condition.

"Tom, what's going on? Is everything alright?"

I didn't know what to say, so I just babbled and said nothing.

"Tom. Tom, you are my hero. I got the whole thing on film," Megan said when she arrived.

Apparently, Megan had checked out one of the Flip cameras from the library that afternoon, and she was playing with it when I walked up to the bar. She thought she'd film me when I returned, but when I didn't come right back, she just kept on filming, and as she did so, the guys at our table were watching her to see what was going on. Apparently, that's why they were able to jump in so quickly when the action started. Later, too, one of the security guys came by to say that they were watching the whole time because Ricardo had been acting pretty strange the whole night, what with arriving late, hanging out in the corners, and not speaking to anyone until I spoke to him at the bar.

Within minutes, Megan, Doreen, and I were sitting at a table with Ms. Cavellari and Tony, and they were all trying to figure out what had just happened. "I am so sorry," I wanted to say, and I wanted to confess everything. Unfortunately, at that moment, I wasn't brave enough or composed enough to say anything, so I listened as the others talked.

"Tell me again who that was," Tony said to Ms. Cavellari.

"He's an old boyfriend from high school. His name is Ricardo."

"And why is he here?"

"I don't know. I think he wants to get back together, but we're done as far as I'm concerned, especially after tonight."

"Were you thinking about getting back together with him?" Megan asked.

"No, not at all." She stopped to think, and it looked like she wanted to say more, so we all waited. "We haven't seen each other in years. He sent me e-mails for a while, and I told him it was over, but he persisted. Finally, I stopped responding." She stopped again and thought for a long while. Finally, she said, "I hoped he would finally get the hint, but I guess he didn't."

Then, Doreen spoke up. "Ms. Cavellari, we haven't met. I'm Megan's friend Doreen. May I ask a question?"

She nodded yes.

"How did he know you were going to be here?"

"I don't know. He actually said something about me inviting him, but I didn't invite him. That is so weird."

At that point, the boat felt like it was slowing down, and we saw red and blue flashing lights outside the window. Megan and I walked to the side and watched as a Troy Police boat pulled up alongside, and the security guys handed Ricardo off to the police. I expected to see him in handcuffs or something, but it looked like he had calmed down and was leaving without a fight. Boy, was I relieved to see him disappear.

Before we returned to the table, Megan whispered: "You know something, don't you?"

"What?"

"Don't lie to me, Tom Sullivan. You are not an innocent bystander in this situation."

I knew she had me, so I just shushed her up and said I would fill her in on everything later. "Just don't throw me in the bag."

"I knew it," she said, as she made a fist and gave a little backward arm thrust, much like Tiger Woods does when he makes a 40-foot putt.

Back at the table, Doreen was deep in conversation with Ms. Cavellari, so I asked Tony if he was okay.

"I am much too old and out of shape for this crazy stuff."

"Definitely crazy, that's for sure."

"So Margaret tells me you're in her Creative Writing class."

"Yeah, she's a great teacher."

"And you're a great writer, apparently."

"She told you that?"

"I'm one of the editors of the student literary magazine, and she told me you had a great poem that she wanted you to submit."

"Yeah, we both like it a lot."

The two of us talked for a while, and he didn't seem like a bad guy after all. Not nice enough that I wanted him to date Ms. Cavellari or anything like that, but he could be her friend. He did stand up to Ricardo after all. I have to give him credit for that.

"Alright, Mr. Sullivan, let's go."

The voice sounded friendly enough, but I couldn't be sure what I was hearing.

"Pardon me?"

"I didn't want to get out on the dance floor with you earlier because of the whole teacher-student thing, but now that you have officially entered my personal life, I think you deserve a slow dance. Let's go."

I couldn't believe it. I had definitely entered her personal life, but not in the way she thought, and I definitely didn't deserve this.

"Really?" I said amazed.

"Now," she answered, "before I change my mind."

Doreen and Tony looked surprised, and Megan looked as if she were pulling out her camera again. I didn't care. In fact, I was thrilled because I couldn't believe this was really happening, and I might need to view the film later on just to prove to myself that it really occurred. I stood up, and Ms. Cavellari actually took my hand and led me to the dance floor.

"I'm not very good at this slow stuff," I admitted.

"Most guys aren't. Don't worry."

The DJ was playing Eric Clapton's "You Look Wonderful Tonight," and I could not have picked a more perfect song. I put my hands around her waist, and she draped her arms over my shoulders and around my neck. What a perfect fit. She was probably two inches shorter than I, and neither one of us said a word. In fact, we barely moved. We danced in a small, little circle. I was tempted to sing along with Eric, but I knew better than that.

Finally, she spoke. "Tom that was pretty brave of you. Thank you."

"You're welcome." I didn't know what else to say.

"So are you interested in Megan or Doreen – or both?"

I laughed. "What do you think?"

"I assumed earlier that it was Megan, but now, I'm not so sure."

"I'm not sure I know myself."

"Really?"

"Really."

"So what are you going to do?"

"I don't know. And what about you and Mr. Masterson?"

"I don't think so."

"Good," I said, and she laughed.

After our dance was over, Tony and Ms. Cavellari returned to the area where all the teachers were sitting, and Megan and Doreen and I returned to sit with the students. The rest of the evening was pretty calm by comparison.

First, Megan showed us the video of the fight on the camera, and I liked what I saw. On film, no one would be able to notice my nervousness or my worry. All they would see is a young guy who boldly and quickly stepped into the middle of a fray to defend his lady's honor. Sort of. Actually, if the viewer didn't know any of the people involved, it probably looked like I was standing up for my friend Tony.

"Could you hear what they said to each other?" Doreen asked as she watched.

With the music playing pretty loudly in the background, it was impossible to hear any conversation on the video, so I tried to reconstruct what I had heard without giving away any of my own involvement.

"I think Ricardo said 'Hello,' and Ms. Cavellari said something about how she was surprised to see him. Then, Tony asked what was going on, and the next thing I knew, Ricardo was knocking Tony to the floor."

"Yeah, but Ms. Cavellari said Ricardo said something about being invited. Did you hear that?"

"I don't remember hearing that line."

Then, Doreen asked another question: "What were you two talking about before the fight erupted."

"Ah, I was just making small talk about the boat."

"What do you think about this whole thing?" Doreen asked Megan. "You're the psychologist."

"Margaret obviously broke Ricardo's heart when she dumped him, and he hasn't gotten over her yet. Happens all the time. No big deal." She paused for a second to click on the next video on the camera. Then, she added, "Here's the big deal," and she played the clip of Ms. Cavellari and me dancing.

We all watched for a few seconds, and Megan laughed and said, "You two are not going to qualify for *Dancing with the Stars*. C'mon, Tom, it's my turn to dance with you."

I knew exactly what she was up to, and she didn't disappoint me once we got on the dance floor. "So what's the whole story? Give it to me now."

"The whole story?"

"The truth, the whole truth, and nothing but the truth, so help me God."

During our three-minute slow dance, I gave her all the details, and her reactions at various points in the story were both surprising and predictable:

"You did what?

"Are you crazy?

"Are you insane?

"You are unbelievable.

"I have to tell Doreen all this."

Naturally, I protested, and she assured me that she was only kidding. "So, what's next?" she asked.

"I don't know," I admitted. "I want to tell Ms. Cavellari everything and apologize, but I'm not sure I can do it. Besides, I'm not sure I should; maybe I should just let it go. What do you think?"

"Oh, no," she said. "Don't drag me into this. As far as what you just told me, I don't know a thing."

"What happened to my helpful psychologist?"

"You need more than a psychologist, believe me."

After we finished dancing, Doreen met me on the dance floor, and said, "My turn!"

So we danced for a while, mostly fast dances, and the three of us spent the rest of the evening hanging out with the other Kennedy College kids, and we all had a good time without anyone getting rip-roaring drunk. By the time the boat pulled back into port, we had worked up an appetite, so Megan and Doreen and I decided to visit the Latham Diner before we headed back to the dorms. And before we exited the boat, we also picked up our five-by-seven photo. We all looked great, so I suggested that we should take turns with the photo, one week at a time, and since I paid for it, they said I could keep it for the first week. As I looked at it later that night, I realized how perfect the photo represented my situation. I had a beautiful girl on each side of me, and at that moment, I couldn't decide which one I liked better.

Sunday, November 14

On Sunday, I followed my normal routine. I slept late, ate lunch, and returned to the room to watch the Jets play a 1:00 game against the Browns in Cleveland. For three and a half hours, I watched the Jets as they played with my emotions. For a good portion of the game, they seemed like they had everything under control. Then, they squandered a few opportunities to put the game away, and they let the Browns tie it and force overtime. In overtime, the Jets missed another chance to win, they looked like they were going to lose, and at the end, it looked like it was going to be a tie. But somehow, at the very end, with about 16 seconds left in the one and only overtime period, Mark Sanchez hit Santonio Holmes on a short crossing route, and somehow, he avoided three defenders and ran 30-plus yards for the winning touchdown. It was amazing! In some ways, the whole experience was even more emotional than the night before – with a lot less at stake, of course.

Later that night, after I had gotten some work done, and against my better judgment, I went into Ms. Cavellari's e-mail account to see if she and Tony had corresponded about their experience the night before. Unfortunately, they hadn't. Or maybe that was a good thing because maybe he figured out, or maybe she told him, that it wasn't going to work between them.

Still feeling that something was up, however, I also logged into her personal e-mail account, and I noticed a long e-mail that she sent to someone at her alma mater with an e-mail address of t.smithson@harvard.edu. This guy must have been some kind of computer expert because she was asking him questions about how hard it would be for someone to hack into her computer account. She explained that she felt someone had gotten into her personal account, and she wanted to know if it were possible to find out, first, if it had really happened, and, second, who this person was.

The person she wrote to responded almost immediately and suggested that she change all of her passwords. Then, he said she should report her suspicions to the administrators of her e-mail account, and though he admitted that he wasn't sure, he felt it was possible for the administrators to track down the offender.

I panicked. I freaked. I worried. I logged off immediately. And I didn't know what to do next. Could they really track me down? Or was this person just blowing smoke to reassure her? If they could track me down, should I live in 24-hour fear and wait for them to catch me? Or should I go in and confess before they caught me? And if I did confess, would they be more lenient on me?

Or better yet, maybe I could use my creative writing skills to come up with a story that would get me out of this jam. I could say I accidentally saw her password (which was true), so I decided to conduct an experiment, and I didn't really mean to forward that e-mail to Ricardo. On paper, that sounded somewhat plausible, but I knew I couldn't pull it off. I'm not that good of an actor. So I decided to do what I do best: nothing.

That's right: nothing. I decided to take my chances. If they caught me, I'd confess at that point and accept my punishment, but if they didn't catch me, I'd simply hang on for dear life. The only other person who knew was Megan, and I trusted her not to turn me in.

Unfortunately, my decision bugged the crap out of me. I couldn't get any work done that night, and I couldn't sleep because I kept thinking about all the possibilities. I needed more information to find out what my chances of getting caught were. So I Googled a bunch of phrases having to do with identity theft, and I received about six gajillion hits, none of which actually answered my question. So I did what Ms. Cavellari had done. I decided to consult my own computer expert.

Just after midnight, I headed over to the computer lab at ACC because I knew Frankie worked Sunday nights. I lied and told him that I thought

I had left my jacket there the previous Wednesday, and, then, I lied again and told him that I was doing a paper on identity theft. (Maybe with all this lying practice, I could actually pull off a creative confession.) Then, I just asked him point blank if it were possible for network administrators to catch someone who was inappropriately using another person's e-mail account.

"Run that by me again," he said.

"Let's say," I explained, "that Student A accidentally leaves his folder in this computer lab and that folder contains both the username and the password of Student A. Then, Student B comes along, finds the folder with that information in it, and Student B logs in as Student A. Is there any way for the network administrators to determine the identity of Student B?"

Frankie rubbed his beard for a bit and thought it over.

"Is this a college e-mail account or a commercial account?"

I pretended to think a bit myself before I answered. "Let's say it's a college account."

Frankie thought about this a bit more. "Is Student B using a college computer to log in, or is he using his own personal laptop?"

"Does it matter?"

"Well, let's see. If Student B logs into the college network as himself but, then, logs into the college e-mail as Student A, the administrators could probably figure out B's identity."

I thought about this for a second and asked, "But what if B logs in as A in both cases? Wouldn't the administrators have to assume that A was simply logging in as himself?"

"I guess so."

"And wouldn't that also be true for a laptop computer?"

"What's the point of your paper again?"

"I'm trying to make the point," I said, and I paused to think of a believable point, "that users should change their passwords frequently because if they don't (another long pause) and if someone else gets a hold of their password, then that other person could read their e-mails and send out other e-mails without the real users knowing about it and without anyone being able to catch the imposter."

"E-mail? Are you kidding me?"

"What?"

"Why would he be reading the student's e-mail when he can probably get into the guy's bank account and steal some money?"

"I thought we said we were talking about a college e-mail account."

"Yeah, but I read somewhere that most people are so lazy – or so stupid – that they use the same username and password for just about everything online."

"Really?"

"What do you do?"

"I have two passwords, and I use one or the other for everything."

"Yeah, and you're supposed to be a smart college guy. So don't you think a lot of people have one password and one password only?"

"I'll have to check my research. So anyway, what's the answer to the question? Would anybody be able to figure out what Student B was up to?"

"It's definitely possible, but it's a real long shot."

"What do you mean?"

"Well, let's just say the information is in there, and it could be tracked down, but if nobody's looking for it . . . ."

"Okay, I get it, but what if Student A is suspicious and reports her suspicions to the authorities?"

"Her suspicions?"

"What?"

"First, Student A was a guy; now, it's a girl. Hey, wait a minute, you ain't writing no paper. You have some girl's e-mail address. Don't you?"

"Don't be a moron. I told you I'm writing a paper."

"And Student A just had a sex-change operation?"

"Look, when you write these papers, you can't be sexist; you have to say 'his or her' all the time; that's all."

"Yeah, I believe that."

"Alright, I don't care what you believe. So what happens once Student A reports that someone has been in the account? Can they track down Student B?"

"It's still a long shot, and it would probably take a long time."

"Tell me more."

"Well, if you use your own laptop on campus to get into this girl's e-mail account, then – ."

"Frankie."

"I'm just saying."

"Go ahead."

"If you use your laptop, they probably can't catch you because you only have a temporary IP address when you log into the network, and once you log off, it's gone."

"But what if I – ."

"Yeah, busted, big guy!"

"It's called sarcasm, you idiot. What if Student B logs in on one of the machines in one of the computer labs?"

"He could get caught doing it that way, but they'd have to be looking for that account to log in, then they'd have to track down the location of the computer, and then, they'd have to get security over there to catch him in the act. So if you're going to keep spying on this girl, you better get on and off quickly. By the way, how'd she find out you were reading her e-mails?"

"I was stupid."

"You didn't?"

"I did."

"You sent out an e-mail on her account? Boy, you are dumber than I thought. Please tell me all about it."

"You can't say a word to anyone."

"I'm like a defective hard drive; once it goes in, it doesn't come back out."

By the time we were finished, Frankie knew everything, and he reassured me that if I just stayed out of her account, they'd never be able to track me down. And once I told him that she was going to change her password, then he was convinced that they couldn't go back in and find me based on what I did in the past. I felt so relieved that I went over to the vending machine in the lab and bought each of us a candy bar.

Monday, November 15

By the time I got back to the dorm, it was pretty late, but at least I could sleep. In fact, I slept so well that I was ten minutes late for Creative Writing class, and when I walked in, some of the guys starting humming the theme song from "Rocky."

"Alright, boys, that's enough," Ms. Cavellari said before they got out of hand.

Apparently, everyone was talking before class about me mixing it up with Ricardo, and they were begging Megan to show them the video. Fortunately, she didn't have the camera with her, and besides, I don't think she'd do that to me.

"Of course, I wouldn't do that to you," she said later when I asked. "I might put it on YouTube, though."

During class, Ms. Cavellari was pressuring us to come up with our video ideas soon. Since most people were struggling as much as I was, we spent a lot of time as a group brainstorming ideas. She stressed that we should figure out our theme first, our main idea, what was really important to us. She mentioned "love" or "fairness" or "perseverance" as possibilities, and we talked about movies we had seen that promoted those ideas.

Then, she said once we had settled on something, we should begin to think about characters, and we should especially begin to think about the conflict between these characters, so we could see how they act under pressure. She said that a character's true self comes out when he is faced with a difficult decision or an ethical dilemma. She added: "It's what he does when he thinks no one is watching that reveals the most about a man."

Then, she suggested, we spend the rest of our time looking at videos online to get ideas.

"Was she talking about me?" I asked Megan afterwards.

"She doesn't know what you did; does she?"

"She could suspect something, no?"

"Yeah, you're right. So when are you going to turn yourself in?"

"I'm not. Frankie, my computer buddy at ACC, says there's no way I can get caught."

"Does this guy know anything?"

"He's an expert. He eats computers for breakfast."

"You better hope he's right."

Later that afternoon, I began thinking about our Thanksgiving break. Usually for Thanksgiving, my mother's family comes over around noon, and we eat about one. Typically, we have 20-25 people. It's a great time. Then, later, around 5:00-5:30, all my dad's relatives drop in, so the place is packed, and we eat again while we watch football. This year will be extra special because the Jets are playing the Thursday night game, against the Bengals, I think. Now if I can just get through this week without any more big assignments coming my way, I'll be okay.

During supper in the cafeteria, I saw Doreen sitting alone, so I went and sat down next to her.

"Hey, we didn't see you this morning. Are you okay?"

"Yeah, but I actually had to go to the hospital because the girl who lives across the hall from us passed out earlier."

"Is she okay?"

"Between you and me, I think she might be anorexic, but she denies it."

"What'd the doctor say?"

"He didn't say anything. He just told her to make sure she gets enough rest and enough food, 'especially during the busy final weeks of the semester.' He was so pompous, it was ridiculous."

After that, we just sat there and talked until everyone else was gone, and the cleaning staff started coming through. We had a great conversation too. She told me she's the oldest child in her family, and she has two younger brothers, one a junior and one a freshman in high school. Her family lives up near the Canadian border in Newton, a real small town that most people have never heard of. She said her town is so small that her graduating class had only 37 kids, and that she was the valedictorian.

The valedictorian part didn't surprise me at all because she seems pretty sharp, but she said that she doesn't feel smart at all here on campus where there are so many smart kids. Despite her worries, she said she's getting mostly A's, but she's never worked so hard in school in her life.

We also talked about all kinds of other stuff, and she asked me about my family. The conversation was so easy, and she's got such a great sense of humor and such passion. In fact, she's still bugging me about my video, so I really do have to come up with an idea and soon.

After we left, I walked her to her dorm, and when I went back to my own dorm, I couldn't help but compare her to Megan. In many ways, they're very much alike, but Doreen seems a little softer and sweeter. Megan's got a bit of an edge to her. They're both attractive, but again, Doreen's got a slight edge with her dimples and her light red hair. I guess that's the Irish side of me coming out. If I had to choose this moment, I think I'd choose Doreen, but it would be a close call. This sounds crazy, but I think I could choose either one of them and be happy. Maybe I should just flip a coin and leave it to the hands of fate. Yeah, there's a mature decision. Good night.

Tuesday, November 16

After such a pleasant dinner and a productive evening of reading and studying for my other courses, I faced a rude awakening in the morning. I got an e-mail from the computer services office. It read:

"Tom,
We have had some e-mail account problems here on campus lately, and we would like to talk to you about your e-mail account in particular. Please come to the Computer Services Building on Thursday, November 18, at 10:00 a.m. Thank you.
Steve Hartley"

Crap! I should have known that Frankie doesn't know what he's talking about. He practically guaranteed me that they couldn't find me, and now I get this. Unbelievable.

My mind started racing immediately. What would they do to me? A warning? A suspension? Expulsion? No, that's way too much. Just for reading someone's e-mail. Okay, just for sending one e-mail on her behalf. And, yes, I guess I did tamper with one of my grades, but I was really just testing the system. I could have raised my grade, and I didn't. And it's not like I purposely stole her e-mail. She accidentally put it out there and practically begged me to do something with it.

"What about just admitting your stupidity and taking your punishment like a man?"

Now my conscience was talking out loud to me.

"And what about 'It's what he does when he thinks no one is watching that reveals the most about a man.'?"

But what if I could get away with it? What if I just lied my way through the whole thing? How would that affect me? Would I just put it behind me and learn my lesson? Or would I be haunted by the whole experience? And how would it affect my relationship with Ms. Cavellari? Or with Megan or Frankie, the people who know the truth?

This is crazy. This is way too much to think about. Do I really have to wait until Thursday? I'll drive myself crazy in the meantime. I have to do something. Maybe I should go for a run. Yes, that's a good idea: burn off some energy and calm down before I take on the rest of the day

So that's what I did. I didn't feel like running on the track or even on the sidewalks or roadways, so I ran to the golf course behind the campus, and I ran the entire 18 holes. I've never done that before. Mid-November, there's nobody out there, of course, so I didn't bother anyone, and all the snow we had received earlier had already melted. I ran straight down the fairways and up to and around the greens. I was afraid I might damage the greens in some way if I actually ran on them because some of them seemed a bit soft and moist. The whole run took less than an hour, and it was a great workout, especially on the hills.

By the time I was done, I had run off some of my nervousness, and I had also come up with an idea for my movie. So after I showered, I called Doreen and asked her if we could start filming later in the afternoon. "Sure," she said. "What's the storyline?"

"I'll tell you later. How about if I pick you up around three-thirty?"

"I have class until four."

"Okay, I'll see you then."

I couldn't give her specific details at that point because I hadn't yet figured them all out. Since I was in the middle of this stupid computer controversy, I wanted to try and explore that idea on film. And I wanted to be behind the camera filming rather than acting, and since Doreen was actually looking forward to the project, I thought I could use her as the main character and simply give her a similar problem to solve.

During religion class, appropriately enough, I had a chance to think more about the problem because we talked about the conflict of man versus society and how at times throughout history, people have had to choose between obeying their God or their government. One student even mentioned the story in the Bible when the people asked Jesus if they should pay taxes to Caesar, and He said something like "give to Caesar what is Caesar's and to God what is God's." Obviously, my situation isn't technically a religious situation, but there's definitely an element of right and wrong.

"So how would you like to be a shoplifter?" I said to Doreen when I picked her up.

"That sounds pretty cool."

"Okay, let's go borrow one of those Flip cameras, and we'll head over to the mall. I know a lot of people who work there, and I'm sure one of them will let us film a scene or two."

As we drove to the mall, Doreen asked me about the main idea, and since I didn't want to let her in on my secret just yet, I simply told her that I wanted to explore the idea of a person doing something wrong for different reasons. I wasn't sure how we were going to communicate the possibilities, but I wanted to film three different scenarios: first, the character shoplifts because she's broke, and she needs to steal; second, because she's bored and just needs the thrill of shoplifting; and, third, because she likes to test herself and wants to see if she can do it without getting caught.

As I thought about those possibilities myself, I compared my e-mail shoplifting to the third option. I didn't really need to see those e-mails; I was just curious. And there really wasn't a big thrill because there wasn't much of a chance of getting caught unless I did something really stupid, which I did, of course. So it definitely had to be the third because I just wanted to see if I could do it, especially the part about the grade changing.

So as I explained the three motives for shoplifting to Doreen, she quickly came up with some great ideas: "For the financial need, we could have her stealing something essential, like bread or milk or a macaroni-and-cheese mix. For the other two, we could have her steal something small and stupid, something that she didn't need at all; we could even somehow show that she actually had the money to pay for it, plenty of money in fact."

"So how do we differentiate between the theft for the thrill and the theft just for the challenge?"

"Maybe we make the second one real easy, like there's nobody watching the store, so to speak, and with the other one, we make it really difficult, so she has to really work at it and overcome some difficulties, like guards or cameras."

"That sounds good."

"So once we film these scenes, what are you going to do with them? Will she get caught? And if she doesn't, will one theft be enough, or will she need more?"

"I don't know. I really don't. I just have a feeling we should film these scenes today, and, later, we'll figure out which one to use and what the next step will be too. Ms. Cavellari always says that 'we can't get from point A to discover point C unless we also work our way through point B.'"

"And what exactly does that mean?"

"She wants us to just keep writing, even if we don't now where we're going with our ideas. She wants us to surprise ourselves, and I feel like that's what's going to happen here too with our filming."

"Okay, let's do it."

I really liked Doreen's idea about stealing food, so we went to the grocery store at the far end of the mall first. Neither one of us saw anyone we knew working there, so Doreen suggested we just ask for permission at the customer-service desk. Once they pointed her to the manager in charge,

Doreen came right out with it. "We're doing a film project for school, so if we buy a few items first, would it be okay if he filmed me pretending to steal those same items later?"

The manager gave Doreen a funny look, but I could tell her dimples were working on him. "I guess that's okay," he finally said, "but I'll have to assign somebody to be with you, so our security guys don't try to arrest you."

"Okay," Doreen said. "That's cool."

"How long will this filming take?"

Not wanting to be entirely left out of the conversation, I jumped in and said, "No more than half an hour tops."

"Alright, why don't you two go buy your products, and I'll find someone to stay with you. And make sure you get a receipt."

I also really liked Doreen's original list of bread, milk, and macaroni and cheese, so we grabbed those, and we also threw in a package of baloney. Then once we had our escort, I started filming. Initially, I had Doreen walking the aisles without a basket or a cart, but Tony, an older guy who was our escort, told us we were doing it all wrong.

"Believe me, I know what I'm talking about," he said. "I've seen some of the best thieves in this store. You want to film her filling up her cart, so she looks like a regular shopper and doesn't stand out. Then, periodically, she slips something in her purse or under her jacket."

"But what happens to the food in the cart? Doesn't that look suspicious if she leaves it all behind?"

"Not if she does it right. The latest scam is to get up near the front of the store with the cart and, then, pretend to receive an important call on a cell phone. It's so important, in fact, that she has to exit immediately and leave the groceries behind. The quiet ones just leave, but the really bold ones actually say that they will be right back. Our security guys are all over that one now, but I'm guessing your average person won't know about it, and it will go over well in your film."

We did exactly what Tony said and filmed the whole thing in less than 20 minutes. Tony really wanted to be in the movie, too, so he convinced us to also film Doreen getting caught. Naturally, Tony played the security guy, and he followed Doreen outside. He was really good too. He made Doreen give everything back, and, then, he yelled at her: "Never step foot in this store again, or I'll call the police."

After that experience, we both knew exactly how to approach the key person at our next store. Doreen suggested we visit one of those cheap jewelry stores they have in every mall, so we could have our main character steal something inexpensive and frivolous. So, when we walked in, Doreen again asked to speak to the manager. When she came out from the small office behind the cash register, Doreen said, "How would you like to be in a movie?"

"Hello, Hollywood," the young girl said with a big smile, and we all laughed. Then, we told her what we were up to, and she even let us go into her office, so we could film from an angle behind the register. And while we were back there, she showed us the video system that they used to keep an eye on their customers. So not only did I film Doreen stealing a 98-cent bracelet from the top of a display case, but I also had her act it out a second time, so I could film the same scene as it appeared on the security system. Then, naturally, we had the manager, Susie, apprehend Doreen in the main hallway just after she exited the store. There, Susie talked to her in a quiet manner, she used her cell phone to call security, and she even escorted Doreen down the hallway to where she knew the security guys hung out: The Donut Shop, of course.

After that performance, I offered to buy Susie a coffee, and we told her more about our project. I explained that Doreen's character could easily afford the bracelet and that she was doing it just for the sake of doing it.

"Have you filmed that scene yet?" Susie asked.

"Which one?"

"The one where you show her having plenty of money."

"Not yet. In fact, I'm not sure we need that scene. I thought the theft of something really cheap would make that point."

"It would," she said, "but the point would be so much stronger if you showed her buying something else with a ton of money in her wallet."

"That's a good idea," I had to admit. Getting these story suggestions from Tony and Susie was amazing. I felt like I was sitting in our Creative Writing class, and my classmates were telling me how to improve my work.

But Susie wasn't just providing ideas; she sprang into action again. "In fact, I'm sure we can film it right here. My friend Ann runs this place, and I'm sure she'd like to be in a movie too."

Within seconds, we were setting up the scene, and Ann was behind the counter about to take Doreen's money for a coffee. When Doreen realized she didn't actually have much money in her purse, I reached into my wallet and pulled out a ten, a five, and two ones.

"That's not enough," Susie said. "Ann, she needs to have a bunch of twenty-dollar bills in there. Can we borrow a few from the register for the sake of the film?"

Ann got a funny look on her face and asked, "You guys aren't setting me up for some *Candid Camera* thing or some reality show, are you?"

"Ann, we've known each other since third grade, and you're asking me that question."

"It's *Undercover Boss*, isn't it? My boss is going to walk in and see me taking twenties out of the register to give to a customer. This little baby camera here is just a front for the real camera, right? Where is it?"

Ann was laughing the whole time, so we knew she was kidding, and she even had Doreen put a fifty-dollar bill on the pile to make it even more impressive. We got what we needed on the first take, but I filmed the scene twice more just in case. We were having a blast with Susie and Ann, and we didn't want to leave, but I still wanted one more scene before we headed back to campus, so we thanked them and headed out. "Good-bye, Hollywood," Susie said with a laugh.

"Let's head down to that place where they sell all that really expensive game stuff," I said to Doreen as we left our new best buddies.

"That video-game stuff?"

"No, that small store where they have the chess board pieces made out of ivory, and they have a marble table with the Monopoly board etched into the table top, stuff like that – stuff that nobody needs and only really rich people can afford."

"They probably won't even let us in there."

"You might be right," I said, but deep down, I knew that even if they rejected me, Doreen's dimples could probably get us in anywhere.

The guy running the store had to be close to 70, but he was real friendly, like an old professor. He looked perfectly at home in this store. Once I explained that we were working on a school project, he said "Yes" immediately. "I went to Kennedy College," he said pointing to the name on the front of my jacket, "and I'm still contributing to the alumni fund, so young whippersnappers like you can learn something there."

"That's so great," Doreen piped in. "I actually made phone calls to the alumni last spring, so maybe we talked on the phone."

"Oh, my darlin'," he said in his best Irish imitation, "that's a beautiful voice you've got there, and I don't think I'd ever forget it if I live to be a hundred."

Doreen actually blushed at that point, and, then, Mr. Chips made us get to work. As we looked at what they had for sale, most of it was too big to steal easily, and most of the small stuff was right next to where Mr. Chips sat. And unlike the jewelry store that was full of young girls and teenagers, this store rarely had any customers, or so it seemed to us.

"I'll tell you what we'll do," Mr. Chips said when we seemed perplexed. "When the next customer walks in, I'll go to the front of the store to talk to him, and you can put one of these outlandishly expensive pen-and-pencil sets in your pocketbook. You should probably turn the box over and look at the price first, so your viewers can see that it cost over $400; they're hand crafted in Brazil."

"Wow!" Doreen and I said in unison.

Fortunately, another older gentleman walked in at that point, so we began acting and filming immediately.

When we finished the theft scene, we asked Mr. Chips if he wanted to be in the film, and he readily accepted. "I would love to co-star with this lovely lass," he said. So we quickly filmed Doreen's entrance to the store and a quick conversation between them before the other customer entered and the theft began.

Doreen and I were both hungry by the time we finished filming, and since I knew the cafeteria would be closed when we got back to campus, I treated Doreen to supper in the food court. As she ate a salad, and I ate my pizza, I noticed that we had barely squeezed in all of our scenes. The video cameras had 60 minutes of filming time, and we had used 58 of them. We were both talking non-stop about our experiences and trying to figure out which scenes would look the best and how we would use them to make our point, whatever it was.

Doreen had been so alive and animated all afternoon. She really was a natural actress, and I complimented her and thanked her profusely.

"Do you think Ms. Cavellari will let me sit in on your class when you show the film?"

"Oh, absolutely. She loves to bring visitors into the classroom. Of course, she may put you on the spot and ask you some questions about the acting process."

"That's okay. I don't mind that at all."

We got back to campus at about 8:45, and after I dropped Doreen off near her dorm, I headed over to the computer lab. I couldn't wait to plug my camera into a computer to download all we had filmed. We had at least two takes of most scenes, so I knew I had plenty to work with. All I had to do was figure out the movie-making program on the system, and I could start this project once and for all. Just getting started finally was a victory, and all that time at the mall had temporarily taken my mind off my own troublesome situation.

In some ways, I felt like my whole life was on hold until I knew what was going to happen to me. This must be how people in jail, or even out on bail, must feel. Everything is up in the air, on hold. I dreaded Thursday, and I couldn't wait for it to come at the same time.

Knowing that working on this film would at least take my mind off Thursday, I began. Ms. Cavellari had showed us briefly how the movie program worked, so I played with it a bit, I used the help screens that were available in the program, and I even found some web sites where they offered tips and directions. I created folders for each of our scenes, and I inserted the takes into the appropriate folders. Once I was sure I had all our filming saved to my account in the system, I deleted our 58 minutes from the camera and returned it to the media reserve section. Since there were a limited amount of cameras and a bunch of students wanting to use them, I didn't want to deprive my fellow directors of their opportunity to film their scenes. I also knew Doreen and I would have to do more filming at some point to finish the project, so I hoped that if I returned my camera promptly, others would do the same for me, and I would have one available when I needed it. Funny how my mind works. I do what I'm supposed to do when I want something in return, but I got myself into this dilemma because I did what I wasn't supposed to do in the first place. On the positive side of this whole crazy situation, I now had a real situation that was worth filming and showing. "Write what you know," Ms. Cavellari says pretty much every day, so that's what I'm doing as I work on this project.

Wednesday, November 17

I arrived early to class on Wednesday, so Megan and I had a chance to talk before class started. "Hey, Doreen told me you guys shot a lot of scenes yesterday. She was really psyched; she said it went real well."

"Yeah, we had a great time, and she's a phenomenal actress. I just give her a general idea of what I'm looking for, and she just goes with it. I can probably show you some of the scenes later if you'd like to see them."

"I would actually because I'm not coming up with any ideas that I like. Maybe your scenes will inspire me."

"Yeah, maybe."

"How's that other thing working out?"

"What other thing?"

"You know what I'm talking about."

"Well, let's just say there's been a complication?"

"What is it?"

I lowered my voice and drew closer to her as I explained what happened.

"Whoa, Tom, I'm sorry. How are you holding up?"

"I've been better; I can tell you that much."

When we finally got in the classroom, a few of our classmates had their videos ready, so we got to see them and comment on them.

The first one was funny and hokey at the same time. Angelo, who plays on the school's football team, made a spoof of some current commercials. They weren't really that funny, but because he had used four or five of the people in this class as his actors, we all got a good laugh. With one of his commercials, for example, he had Molly dress up with a wig and an outfit that makes her look like a woman who was about 40 or 50 years old and complaining about all of her aches and pains. Once she buys and uses the new anti-aging cream, however, everything changes. In the next scene, Molly is her regular, beautiful, 20-year-old self, so not only does she look much younger, but she's also dancing like a wild woman on the dance floor at Vapors up in Saratoga. Silly, right? And that was probably his best one.

Ms. Cavellari was wonderful, as always, and she and everybody else gave Angelo lots of positive feedback, but Megan and I were looking at each other and making faces. I definitely knew mine would be better than that, and I felt Megan could probably take a camera at that moment and come back in an hour with something that was a bit more thought provoking. Ms. Cavellari, though, was so happy because Angelo had volunteered to go first, and I think she was trying to make the process as painless as possible, so the others wouldn't be nervous or intimidated by sharing their work.

Erin went next, and her film was the best of the three. She did kind of a mini-documentary on her grandfather who is now confined to a wheelchair in a nursing home. She introduced him and interviewed him at the beginning, and it was pretty obvious and sad to see that he was near the end. His speech was slurred, she had to repeat her questions, and he appeared as if he might doze off at any time. After that, though, she flashed back to his youth, and she had all kind of pictures of him and even some home movies of his high-school football games. He looked like he was the big man on campus with a great build and a huge smile. Then, after that, she showed him in his Army uniform in what looked like Korea. And later, we saw him doing all kinds of construction work, we saw clips of his wedding, we saw him holding babies, and on and on throughout his whole life. Every once in a while, too, Erin's film would flash back to a recent picture of him in the nursing home. The whole thing was really powerful because we saw all the stages of this man's life, yet we know where he's going to end up before he dies. Some of the girls were crying just watching it, and Ms. Cavellari couldn't help but rave even more about this one. "This is a beautiful presentation, Erin, of the cycle of life and of the universal experiences we will all share." I had a feeling neither Megan nor I would top that one.

The last one was more like a bad music video. Sharon filmed herself and a couple of her roommates singing "Girls Just Want to Have Fun" as they pranced around the campus doing all kinds of goofy stuff like climbing trees, splashing in puddles, and playing on the swing set at a nearby park. Later, she explained that she was trying to show how even though modern girls want to pretend to be mature and sophisticated, they are really just little kids at heart. When she explained it that way, it did make sense, but when I viewed the film on its own, I didn't make that connection, and Ms Cavellari has been harping on this idea that the film should stand on its own without an explanation. So from that perspective, I don't think it worked as well as it could have.

When class was over, I showed Megan a bunch of our clips, and I think she was really impressed. "Is this whole shoplifting thing connected to your computer situation?" she asked.

"Yes, but no one else is going to know about that particular aspect. As far as everyone else is concerned, I'm trying to explore the motivations for why people do what they do, especially things that they shouldn't be doing."

"Do you know where you're going with this?"

"Not yet, but I'm hoping to play with it a lot more at work tonight."

Later, I thought Megan and I might have lunch together, but she said she got a film idea during class today, so she wanted to get started on it. She wouldn't tell me what it was though. "You'll see it soon enough," she said as she took off.

That night at work, I called Frankie and told him about the e-mail I received and about my upcoming meeting.

"They're bluffing," he said. "They got nothing on you. Don't admit to anything."

"So why did they pick me?"

"I don't know what they're doing, but I don't think you should be worried."

"Yeah, that's what you told me last time, and look what happened."

"What, now you're blaming me because you're in trouble?"

"Nah, it's just . . . I don't know."

"Trust me; they got nothin'. Just go in there all innocent and confident and play stupid, which, by the way, should be easy for you."

As I began working on my movie, I decided not to use the grocery-store scene because I didn't want the character's motivation to be that easy. Most people would probably steal food if they were hungry. No big story there.

I did decide to use The Donut-Shop scene with the money and both of the other theft scenes. As Susie suggested, I wanted to make it clear that Doreen's character had more than enough to make her purchase in the jewelry store. Then, I also wanted to show that this character was not satisfied with stealing a 98-cent bracelet from a crowded and busy store. She definitely wanted a bigger challenge, so she moved up to the bigger theft. Then, I had a crazy idea.

What if Doreen's character feels remorse for what she did, so she decides to return the expensive pen-and-pencil set? What would happen to her then? Would she be able to return it just as easily as she stole it? Would she get away with the return? And is the risk of getting caught while returning the set worth more than the fact that she already got away with the theft in the first place?

And obviously, that's exactly what I was doing with my own situation. I felt bad for what I had done, and I wanted to correct the problem, but I didn't want Ms. Cavellari or the college administrators to know what I had done. I wanted to start over with a clean slate. Was that possible? Was it realistic?

When I called Doreen and told her the idea, she said she liked it, and, yes, she would be able to go back there the next day to film the follow-up scene. "Will she get caught?" Doreen asked.

"Probably," I answered, "but I'm not sure."

After Doreen hung up, I also struggled with the soundtrack for the film. We had a bit of dialogue in The Donut Shop, but the rest of the sound was pretty much crowd noise in the mall. I didn't think that would be interesting enough, and I wasn't sure what to use. So I spent the rest of my shift watching music videos and watching videos on YouTube. Some were really good, and some made me sleepy.

To avoid actually falling asleep on the job, I completed one last task that I had been curious about for a few days. I googled Ms. Cavellari's friend Ricardo to see what happened to him after our experience on the cruise. I guess I had assumed that the Troy Police would just bring him back to his car at the dock and tell him to go home to Boston. Boy was I wrong!

Apparently, they ran a check on his driver's license, and they found out that it had been suspended in Massachusetts for driving under the influence of alcohol – twice. Then, they also discovered that as part of his probation from jail, he wasn't supposed to leave the state unless he had permission from his probation officer. I got a bit of a chuckle out of that one. I could just imagine Ricardo saying to the probation officer: "If it's okay with you, I would like to drive to Troy, New York, to surprise my ex-girlfriend, who doesn't really want to see me, and perhaps I will beat up any guy who happens to be with her."

"Sure, no problem. Go ahead. Just drive carefully, so they have no reason to check your suspended license."

As a result, Ricardo was back in jail. One article said he would likely be there for at least three years for the license offense and the probation violation, and he could, in fact, get another two years for his assault on Tony Masterson. Wow!

As a result, Ms. Cavellari wouldn't have to worry about Ricardo for a while, so I felt pretty good about that outcome. But despite that good news, I was feeling even more guilty by the second. If I hadn't forwarded that e-mail, Ricardo would never have known about the cruise or Ms. Cavellari's going on the cruise with another guy. Now granted, Ricardo may have done something equally stupid at some point, but if he did, I wouldn't be involved. And I wouldn't be facing my own firing squad.

The news of Ricardo depressed me more than anything, and combined with working all night, I just wanted to go back to the dorm and take a short nap. Actually, I felt like I wanted to sleep for 20 years like Rip Van Winkle. I could wake up in 2030, I'd be 41 years old, and this ridiculous situation would be long forgotten. Of course, I knew that even a short nap wouldn't be good. What if I slept through my appointment? Would that make me appear guilty? Or innocent? Actually, it didn't matter. There's no way I could postpone the meeting even one day. I had to get this thing out in the open and done with once and for all.

Thursday, November 18

So by 9:45, I was walking into the Computer Services Building and looking for some guy by the name of Steve Hartley. The map inside the front door of the building pointed me down the hallway to the main office. I saw a guy standing outside the door, and he was dressed in a blue dress shirt with a tie, and he had a clipboard in his hand. "Are you Tom Sullivan?"

"Yes."

"Hi, I'm Steve Hartley," and he shook my hand like it was some kind of a business meeting. "We're having a major issue with our backup server right now, so with all the technicians in there, I thought you and I could meet in one of these empty classrooms."

"Okay."

He led the way down the hall, and he passed two empty classrooms before he ushered me into the last classroom on the right. I assumed he would sit at the teacher's desk, but, instead, he pulled two student desks together over by the window, and he motioned for me to sit down. He began shuffling through some papers, and he pulled out a folder with my name on the front before he began to speak.

"Okay, Tom, as I mentioned in the e-mail, we've been having some issues here on campus with individual e-mail accounts, and it looks like yours is one of the accounts affected. Have you noticed any problems on your end?"

"No, I haven't had any problems." I was actually surprised by the beginning of this meeting; I assumed there would be more people involved, and I guess I thought I would be accused of tampering right off the bat.

Maybe Frankie was right. Maybe they didn't have anything on me. Maybe I should just play stupid; he did say I was good at that. Hoping to get more information out of this guy, I asked a question in return.

"What kind of problems are we talking about?"

"Well, sometimes the log-out icon on the computers in the labs hasn't been working properly, so as a result, people think they're logged off, and they walk away, but since the log-out function didn't catch, their account is still open when another user sits down at the computer. Have you seen any unusual activity in your e-mail account or any tampering with the files in your space on the network?"

"No, I haven't noticed a thing."

"Okay, that's good." He was taking notes as we spoke, so we had a bit of a pause before he spoke again. During the pause, I could feel my stomach tighten, and I began to anticipate the questions that were coming next.

"Have you ever sat down at a computer in the lab and noticed that the previous user did not log off?"

"I haven't seen it happen very often here at Kennedy, but I used to see it all the time over at ACC."

"What do you mean?"

"I worked in the computer lab over there; in fact, I still work over there one night a week."

"And?"

"And lots of freshmen forget to log off, especially during the beginning of the semester."

"So, how do you handle that when it happens?"

"If they're still nearby when we notice, we try to catch them and explain to them how important it is to log off, so no one else can go into their account." I actually began to relax a bit because I was telling the truth, and Steve wasn't even looking at me. He was still taking notes. Maybe I could pull this off after all.

"And what if they're not nearby; what if they're long gone when you discover they haven't logged off."

"Then, I just log them off and move on."

"You've never been tempted to look at their documents or pictures?"

"I might see things accidentally if they leave a file open or if I see a picture on their screen saver."

"And when that happens?"

"I close the file or the web page, whatever they were looking at when they left, and I log them off." My nervousness began to return, and I could feel my mouth getting dry. He paused for a second, still writing, and, then, he looked up. He looked me straight in the eye.

"Tom . . . ." He paused again and rubbed his chin with his left hand. I waited.

"Okay, I admit it. I did it. I'm guilty, and I'm sorry, and I promise not to do it again."

"Pardon me?"

I couldn't play stupid. I couldn't lie. I couldn't even wait out the whole process. I just wanted to confess and move on, whatever the consequences. Quite honestly, I was hoping for leniency for telling the truth up front, but I was ready to accept whatever punishment they dished out.

"I accidentally came across my teacher's password, and I went into her e-mail account on numerous occasions. Believe me, I'm not a hacker, and I wasn't trying to do anything wrong. I'm just a stupid college student, and I made some mistakes in judgment."

"But, you obviously have some computer expertise. Otherwise, you wouldn't be working in a computer lab."

"Yeah, but my expertise is really limited. I show new students how to log in. I show them how to use e-mail. I show them how to use word processing and PowerPoint, but that's about it. I can't even answer Excel questions because I've never actually taken a computer class myself. I'm really just a warm body whose responsibility is to fix the staplers and keep the printers filled with paper."

"What else did you look at besides e-mail?"

"I looked at Word files. I looked at pictures. I went into Facebook. I even went into her gradebook for our class."

"You mean this teacher used the same password for all of those accounts."

I shook my head, "Yes."

"Boy, that's not very smart," and we both shared a minor laugh. Then, he hesitated a bit, and asked, "Did you change any of your own grades?"

"I did, but, and I know this will be hard to believe, I lowered one of my grades."

"You lowered a grade?"

"Stupid, right. It's just that I'm doing okay in that class, so I didn't need any help, but I wanted to see if it were possible."

He looked at me for a long time, and I thought I saw a sign of lenience on his face, so I apologized again.

"Believe me; I've learned my lesson. I've been a nervous wreck since I got your e-mail, and I promise I will never do anything like this again. You have my word."

"Okay, Tom. I guess that's all I need to know right now. I will have to report all of this to my superiors, and I will get back to you by early next week with our decision."

"How bad could it be?"

He exhaled deeply and looked over his notes again before answering. "Well, on the positive side, you did confess, and you do appear to be remorseful. You haven't yet been in any trouble here at Kennedy College, and your community-college record is spotless, so I'm guessing they'll take all of that into consideration." He paused again to think, and I waited. "However, you must understand that we cannot let these types of things go unpunished."

I nodded. I understood perfectly.

"So while I don't think you'll get off completely, I also don't think you'll be expelled from the college; your punishment will be somewhere between those two extremes. And if I had to guess, it will be closer to the side of mercy. However, you will probably be placed on notice for a period of time, so that if you do get into any more trouble during that probationary period, you will face much more serious consequences."

I nodded again. My throat was completely dry, and I didn't have anything to say anyway.

"Do you have any questions before I let you go?"

"No," I replied by shaking my head.

"Okay, you can go," he said. "As I mentioned, you should get our decision early next week by e-mail. If that changes or if I need to see you again, I will contact you."

At that point, he stood up, so I did too. He shook my hand again and thanked me for being so "forthright." I wasn't sure if I should wait for him or leave on my own until he spoke again. "I'm just going to stay here and finish up my paperwork. You don't have to wait for me."

Boy, was I relieved when I left. I felt good about confessing everything rather than trying to play any games, and I was optimistic about my punishment. I felt like maybe I'd get a stern warning and some sort of probation, but I was no longer worried about getting kicked out of school, especially since I didn't really steal anything or hurt anybody. I was a little surprised, though, that Ms. Cavellari's name never came up, and that he didn't really give me a hard time about what I had done. I at least expected a stern lecture about respecting others' rights and doing unto others, that sort of thing. Not that I was disappointed. Exhausted by the whole experience, I went back to the dorm and slept all the way through lunch.

Around mid-afternoon, I called Doreen to see if she could go with me to film that scene we had discussed earlier. She said she was ready, so I stopped, first, at the library to pick up a camera and, then, at her dorm. As we drove to the mall, I explained that I had missed lunch, and she said she had plenty of time, so we could stop at the food court again if I wanted before we began filming. Though she said she wasn't too hungry, we both ate some pizza as I tried to explain her character's motivation.

"Initially," I explained, "this character has low self-esteem, so she steals just to prove to herself that she can do what most people cannot: steal and get away with it. After her success, however, her conscience kicks in, and she wants to return the stolen item to relieve her guilt. She knows it's a bit of a risk, but she's so confident that she can do it, she proceeds despite the danger."

"This is one messed up girl I'm playing."

"Fortunately, you're a good actress."

About 20 minutes later, we made our way to the scene of the crime, and, fortunately, Mr. Chips was working.

"Ah, my beautiful maiden," he said when he saw Doreen, "and her ugly big brother," when he saw me. He was sincerely glad to see us, and he said he hoped we might return.

"Are you so glad," asked Doreen, "that you're still willing to be in our film?"

"Of course."

Within minutes, Mr. Chips and Doreen were blocking out the scene, and they sent me to find one of the security guards. There were none in The Donut Shop, so I actually had to hike through the mall before I found one. When I explained what I needed, he was more than willing to help, but he said he had to clear it with his supervisor. So as we walked back to the store, he called his boss and secured permission. "Thank you for finding me," he laughed. "This job is so boring."

Once we actually started filming, I only needed three takes before I was convinced that we had what we needed. In the first take, Mr. Chips didn't say a word. He simply grabbed Doreen by the arm, escorted her to the hallway, and handed her over to the security guard who just happened to be there. In the second take, he treated her as if he were a gentle grandfather chastising his granddaughter for breaking a glass at the dinner table, and, then, he called security. Then, in the final take, he really got into it and raged at her, almost as if he were losing control, and again, he escorted her to the hallway where he made a big scene until security arrived. I think the people in the hallway all thought it was real because the place got deathly quiet until I finished filming, and Doreen, Mr. Chips, the security guy, and I all burst out laughing.

When we finished, we went back to Mr. Chips' store and just hung out with him for a good half hour. Even the security guy joined us. I played back all three takes for them to see, and Mr. Chips enjoyed them so much, he had me download them to his computer in the back room, so he could show them to his wife at some point.

Afterwards, we drove back to campus, and I actually filmed a few more scenes of Doreen in her dorm room. I wanted to show her experiencing some guilt over stealing the pens, and Doreen had been smart enough to ask Mr. Chips for a similar gift box that we could use to show she possessed the stolen property for a while before she tried to return it. This time, I filmed a total of about 40 minutes.

When I finally put the camera away, Doreen again told me how much she enjoyed acting out those scenes, and she thanked me for the experience. "I really need to get involved in the theater club next semester," she said. "I really miss acting, and I need to do more of it."

Personally, I wanted to spend a bit more time with her, but she said she had a lot of work to do before she left for Thanksgiving break. Naturally, I did too, but I would have sacrificed something to work things out. So while she stayed in her room to work, I headed over to the computer lab to download my scenes and begin the final project.

I also began to work on a philosophy paper that was due Monday, and the topic of this assignment also seemed to connect with my film project. I had to write about Socrates and his "Allegory of the Cave." Though I don't feel like I truly understand the whole thing, I think I do understand the basic premise of his parable. When the people in the cave were first looking at the shadows, they thought the shadows were real. But afterwards, when they saw the real beings who created the shadows, they realized that what they had seen earlier was a distortion of reality. At that point, I get lost regarding the overall message, but I do see a parallel with my situation.

At first, I thought it would be fun and harmless to explore Ms. Cavellari's computer account, but that idea was distorted. In fact, I was invading her personal and private space where I was neither invited nor wanted. Thus, I definitely needed to be caught, to be made aware of reality, so I could appreciate my previous ignorance. The more I wrote on the subject, the more I realized that I might also be able to use some of this stuff in my film project. Maybe I could film some shadows, or maybe I could narrate some of Socrates' words. That would definitely give my film a certain intellectual angle, one that I'm not sure it had in its current rough format. Since my film was also due on Monday, I was pleased that I could combine these two tasks in a small way.

Friday, November 19

During Creative Writing class on Friday, we viewed more films, and one of them was really well done. Two students, Amy and Todd, had teamed up to do a joint film, and they decided to name their film "First Kiss." These two have been dating since their first day on campus, so they starred as themselves in the film, and they both also filmed themselves walking together. Each of them borrowed two cameras and set them up on tripods, so they got the same scene from four different angles. One camera filmed them from behind, another filmed them as they walked toward that second camera, and the two others filmed them from the sides. I'm guessing the total distance was no more than 20 yards, but a lot happens in that small space.

First, the audience sees the couple walking slowly down one of the campus walkways, and the space between them is a foot or a foot and a half. They're obviously enjoying one another's company because they're looking at each other, talking, and laughing. Then, she stumbles just a bit, and he reaches out to steady her. His right hand catches her left elbow, and they keep walking. They are much closer, and his hand has slid down to hold hers. They walk even more slowly, and their conversation has come to a halt. They look at each other for a few steps, and, then, he comes to a stop. Her momentum carries her forward a step, but he pulls her back. They tentatively embrace. She looks downward as if she she's too shy to look up at him, so he gently caresses her hair. She slowly raises her eyes to him. They hold that position for a few seconds before they both lean forward. Finally, they kiss, the gentlest kiss ever. She closes her eyes, and he smiles just a bit. The film closes with that sweet shot.

All the girls were cooing when the film finished, and even the guys were impressed. The whole experience in real time probably took only 10 to 15 seconds, but they used slow motion and the footage from all four cameras to make a two-minute film. Naturally, they had romantic music accompanying the scene, and it started slowly and built to a soft but powerful crescendo.

Ms. Cavellari loved it, and she wanted more people to see it. "Maybe we should organize a public showing of these films," she said to the class, and most people responded positively.

"Yes, that would be so cool."

"Yeah, let's do it."

"We'll call it the Kennedy Awards . . . or maybe just the Kennys."

I really liked the idea, too, and everybody was buzzing about where and when we should show the films.

"Well, definitely not until after the Thanksgiving break," Ms. Cavellari said, and as she spoke, I began feeling anxious and nervous again. I knew I really needed to do a lot of work on my film if I were going to have a public viewing. It's one thing to show it in class but another thing altogether to show it in front of a real crowd. The possibility thrilled me and scared me simultaneously.

And Doreen would absolutely love it, I thought. It might be good for her, too, because other people on campus would see what a good actress she is, and that might open up some possibilities for her.

"Megs, what do you think," I asked.

"Boy, I don't know."

"Really? Why?"

"I don't know if my film is going to be that good."

"Ah, I don't believe that for a second. Which reminds me, am I going to see your film beforehand, or do I have to wait, like everyone else, until Monday's class?"

"Monday."

"Alright, you can't see my finished product until then either."

"It's a deal," she said, and she reached out and shook my hand.

Before I let go of her hand, I asked her out: "How would you like to do something tomorrow night?"

"Sure. What do you have in mind?"

"How about dinner and a movie? A good film might inspire us."

"I'll let you pick the restaurant if you let me pick the movie."

"You must already have one in mind."

"I do."

"And that movie is . . . ?"

"*Secretariat*. I just love horses."

"Okay. I've heard that's a good movie. Let's do it. I'll pick you up about seven o'clock, if that's okay."

"I'll see you then."

I wasn't sure how she would react. I wasn't even sure if I'd have the confidence to ask her out. Yet, the conversation had been so easy. We've hung out together a lot, but we've never gone on a date like this. Actually, I have been trying to decide between Megan and Doreen, and after all the time I've spent with Doreen lately, I'd been leaning in her direction. Before I commit, though, I wanted to spend at least one evening with Megan, so this is it.

Saturday, November 20

During the afternoon before our date, I spliced together all the shots that I wanted for my movie, and I pretty much figured out how to use Movie Maker. It really wasn't that difficult once I got the key concepts down. Now, I just have to add a soundtrack. I was tempted to ask either Doreen or Megan to help me, but since Megan was going to make me wait to see her film, I had to do the same; and since I was seeing Megan later, I was afraid that if I spent more time with Doreen, I'd get all hung up on her again. Bottom line: I guess I'll have to do the soundtrack on my own.

For dinner, I decided on Ruby Tuesday because they have good food and because it's in the same mall as the movie theater. Whenever I go out to eat before a movie, I'm always afraid I'm going to miss the movie because the restaurant is too crowded, or the service is too slow, or because I get stuck in traffic moving from the restaurant to the theater. I know it's stupid, but I find myself constantly looking at my watch, so I don't enjoy the meal as much as I should. By choosing a restaurant in the mall, I figure I will at least eliminate the traffic problem.

Naturally, the restaurant was packed on a Saturday night, but I also had the good sense to make a reservation. Thus, Megan and I were seated and ordering food with plenty of time to eat and still make it to the theater on time. During dinner, we both told a lot of stories about our past, and Megan teased me about everything. That's one of the things I really like about her. She's got a great sense of humor, and she won't let me take myself too seriously.

She told me that she acquired her sense of humor from six older siblings: three boys and three girls. As the baby of the family by seven years, she says her brothers and sisters definitely spoiled her, but they also treated her like an adult, so she matured quickly, and she was always present for all their activities: concerts, games, parties, and pranks, especially pranks. She said her favorite prank occurred when she was in eighth grade. After always driving a clunker while the kids were growing up, her father finally went out and got himself a new sporty car with a sun roof. He was all excited to drive it to the golf course the following Saturday, but after he put his clubs in the trunk and opened the front door, he noticed that the car was filled entirely with styrofoam peanuts. Apparently, one of her brothers worked at a shipping warehouse, and they decided to open the sun roof and fill the inside with the peanuts. Fortunately, her dad has a good sense of humor, too, and he didn't blow up at the boys for what they had done. She said her dad does get annoyed, however, when he still finds peanuts in the nooks and crannies of his car almost seven years later.

Later, as we sat in the theater waiting for the movie to begin, Megan also told me about her fascination for horses. Since her family was too big and too poor to be able to afford riding lessons for her, she volunteered to work at a local horse farm in return for lessons. She said the farm owners made her clean out the stalls for two weeks before they even allowed her anywhere near the horses. They were testing her desire, she said, and she was determined to succeed. After two weeks, they let her brush the horses, and after two weeks of that, she finally got her first ride. She was never able to ride enough to be able to compete or anything like that, but she loved the animals nonetheless, and she said she would like to own one or two horses of her own when she finally gets her own place.

The movie itself was really good. Since I already knew the horse's history, I wasn't confident the story would be able to hold my interest for two hours, but it definitely did. One of the scenes actually took place locally in Saratoga, though I'm not sure if they filmed it there. And did I mention that the beautiful Diane Lane played the main character, the woman who owned Secretariat? Yes, I know she's a lot older than I, even a lot older than Ms. Cavellari, but she's so good looking, and I've seen her in a few movies: *Nights of Rodanthe*, *Must Love Dogs*, and a few others that I can't remember at the moment.

Megan especially loved the film not only because of the horses, but also because Diane Lane's character plays such a strong female lead. I think Megan really identifies with strong females, and that's one thing, I have to admit, that scares me a bit about her. I'm not really sure I'm strong enough to handle her. Sure, we get along in class and when we hang out, but what would happen if we actually were in a serious relationship together? Would she overwhelm me? Would I be strong enough to stand up to her? Would I be willing to argue and battle with her if I had to?

I'm not really an argumentative type, and I usually let others have their way rather than fight things through. I know I need to work on that, but one of the things I like about Doreen is the fact that she's so easygoing, even more than I am. I think that's good, but maybe that would get tiresome too. Who knows?

After the movie, Megan and I went back to Ruby Tuesday for a drink. The place was packed, so we bumped into lots of people we knew either from school or from our hometowns. The girl behind the bar said they usually slow down after the main dinner hour, but that the weekend before Thanksgiving is always busy because a lot of college kids come home for the break. As a result, I met a few of Megan's old high-school buddies, and she met a few of my old classmates. By the time I brought her back to campus, it was about 2:30, and we were both pretty whipped. If she had invited me to stay for a while, I would have been re-energized, but that didn't happen. I think we both had a good time, but I think we both also knew that we were definitely still in the friend stage and trying to find out if the relationship was going to go any further. I was hopeful and optimistic, and she seemed somewhat interested. But we definitely weren't there yet.

After I left her dorm, I drove off campus to pick up some cookies and milk. Even though I was tired, I was craving some chocolate-chip cookies and a cold glass of milk. And when I got back to my room, Teddy was still awake and working on one of his term papers. This guy is dedicated, believe me. Since we hadn't seen each other in a while, we talked for an hour or so, and he was grateful to share my late-night snack. Though we don't see each other that often, he really is a good guy, and he seems genuinely interested in my activities. I didn't feel comfortable enough to tell him about my computer problem, but I did tell him about Doreen and Megan. When I described them to him, he gave me his own personal advice on women:

"Definitely go with Doreen."

"Definitely Doreen? Why do you say that?"

"Because even an easygoing girl is going to be a lot of work, and I'm not sure an easygoing guy like you wants to work that hard."

"So is that advice based primarily on me or on those two types of women in general?"

"Actually, it's more about the women."

"And you're basing that advice on your own personal experience?"

"Well, not dating experience per se but a certain type of experience. I've seen a lot of the Megan types in my classes and at work, and they're pretty serious and driven and not very flexible or open to the ideas of others."

"So you think these women will be equally driven and inflexible in their personal relationships?"

"I do. In fact, I can tell you that my mom is driven and inflexible, and she can be a bear to live with. Everything has to be a certain way – her way, of course – and that can wear you down after a while. Just ask my dad."

"So, are you a little bit like your mom?"

"I definitely am – which may explain why I haven't had a date in a while."

"So if it doesn't work out with me and Megan, do you want her number?"

"Maybe . . . . Maybe, I do."

Sunday, November 21

Okay, I am officially addicted to football, specifically New York Jets football. Sundays used to mean getting up and going to church in the morning. That hasn't happened in a while. Now, I sleep late, get up and have lunch, and, then, I settle in for a 1:00 football game. And I don't want to miss a single play. My Sunday afternoon revolves around the three to three and a half hours when the game is on, and my trips to the kitchen and to the bathroom have to occur during commercial breaks. I won't answer the phone, and I don't want anybody to drop in on me unless they want to sit down and watch the game with me. Am I pathetic or what?

Yes, I am pathetic, but I have good reason. The Jets are seven and two so far this year, and the two games they lost were so close: by a single point, 10-9, to the Ravens, and the Jets had a chance to win at the end; and to the Packers by nine points, 9-0, in a game where neither team scored a touchdown. So, the Jets definitely have a great chance of doing something special this year. Is it really possible and realistic to say the words "Super Bowl"? Yes.

Sure, they have won some close games recently to mediocre teams, but in the past, they would have lost those games, so that's a real positive sign. And today's game was pretty much the same. They played the Houston

Texans who were four and five coming into New York, and the Jets were favored by six or seven. The first half was pretty even, but by the beginning of the fourth quarter, we were comfortably ahead by 16, 23-7. At that point, I actually thought about turning the game off because I figured we had it under control. It was a beautiful, fall, Sunday afternoon, and I thought about just going outside for a walk. But I didn't. I couldn't get up from the couch, and the next thing I knew, we fumbled, they scored a touchdown, and soon they scored again with a field goal. Our lead was down to 23-17. I still felt pretty confident, but the defense and the offense faltered.

First, the Texans scored a touchdown to go ahead 24-23 with about two minutes left. Okay, we can still go down the field and kick a field goal. But that's when Mark Sanchez got hit while throwing, and they intercepted. At that point, I assumed it was over, especially when they kicked a field goal to go ahead 27-23 with 40 seconds left. A win didn't seem possible at that point unless we got a huge kickoff return. We didn't, so seven and two was looking like seven and three. Approximately 80 yards in 40 seconds with no timeouts. Couldn't happen. But it did.

Somehow Mark Sanchez hit two short passes to LaDainian Tomlinson, he spiked one pass to stop the clock, and then he hit Braylon Edwards down the right sideline for about 40 yards. With about 16 seconds left, we were first and goal, and on the very next play, Sanchez hit Santonio Holmes in the right corner of the end zone for the winning touchdown. Unbelievable. Un-be-lieve-able! I am so glad I did not go for a walk. That was definitely the most exciting comeback I have ever seen.

I was so excited afterwards that I knew I had to do something physical, so I went to the gym and played pickup basketball for an hour or so. And I was on fire. The gym was packed with guys playing five-on-five on all four courts. I played with a group of guys from our dorm, and we did not lose because I could not miss. It was just one of those days when everything I threw up toward the rim went in. I was in the zone. I was feeling it. And what a great feeling that was. It didn't matter if I was wide open or if a guy was hanging all over me; I just knew my shot was going to hit nothing but net. "You just keep shooting, Hooper," one of my older teammates said to me after I hit my fourth or fifth shot in a row. What a rush that was. No one had ever called me "Hooper" before.

By the time I finished eating and got all showered and cleaned up, the last thing I wanted to do was school work, but I had no choice. I had to finish my philosophy paper and my movie. Fortunately, my sports rush had inspired me, so I hustled over to the computer lab in the library. Since

I knew finishing the film would be more fun, I forced myself to do the philosophy paper first. It took about two hours, but I finally got that done, and then I played with the movie and its soundtrack for another two hours before I felt satisfied. Was it good enough for a Kenny? I wasn't sure, but I looked forward to showing it in class the next day. I went to sleep that night exhausted and exhilarated by the day's events. And my dreams were amazing.

Monday, November 22

I don't really think dreams have any meaning whatsoever, but I do enjoy the good ones. Obviously, the scary ones are not fun, so if I wake up in the middle of the night during a scary dream, I always get up and wash my face, so I don't return to that bad dream. When I wake up during a good dream, however, I try to get back to sleep as quickly as I can. And I had some good dreams last night.

Because I ran cross country for four years in high school and spent so much time training, I find that running is a recurring dream. Sometimes, I'm really moving, almost flying, and sometimes, I can barely move my legs. Those slow nights aren't necessarily scary, but they are frustrating. These dreams were not frustrating at all.

I was really moving down the final stretch of the race, and Megan, Doreen, and even Ms. Cavellari were cheering me on. I was feeling so confident that as I easily passed the runners in front of me, I winked at the girls and motioned for them to meet me at the finish. There, with a trophy in my hand, the race organizers placed a wreath on my head, and a photographer from the local newspaper took a picture of me and the three girls. I was in heaven, definitely heaven. I did not want to wake up. And even after I did wake up, I stayed in bed for about 15 minutes and re-lived the whole experience.

Was the dream some kind of an omen? As I said earlier, I don't usually believe such things, but I really wanted to believe this one, especially the part about all three girls cheering me on. Maybe I could date both Megan and Doreen. Or maybe I really was destined to be with the magnificent Margaret Cavellari. Oh, what a dreamer!

During philosophy class, Mr. Matthews collected our papers, and, then, he had each of us go to the front of the room to talk about what we had written. He didn't tell us beforehand that he was going to do that, but since the information was still pretty fresh in my mind, the task was pretty easy. In fact, I was surprised that some of my classmates struggled so much with it, and, then, I realized what Mr. Matthews was up to.

I think he was trying to figure out beforehand who had really written their own papers and who had plagiarized. I know some students blatantly copy and paste from the internet, and I even know one guy who admitted that he actually purchased a paper from one of those term-paper web sites. He said he paid a hundred dollars for it, the teacher never suspected a thing, and the teacher gave him an 88. Part of me was amazed when I heard that story, and part of me was upset. I was amazed that he could actually get away with that, and I was upset that he did. I began to wonder how many other students were cheating like that, ripping off the system. Normally, I don't feel like I'm competing with my classmates, and normally it doesn't bother me when I see other students using cheat sheets during tests. In fact, I have to admit, that I, too, have cheated on tests once or twice, usually when the work is well beyond me or when for some reason I didn't get a chance to study. Obviously, I can't justify what I did, but somehow buying a term paper feels like crossing the line. At least with cheating, I have to prepare my own cheat sheet, or I have to be bold enough and sneaky enough to copy off someone's paper. But just ordering a paper online and using a credit card to pay for it? That's going too far.

Since I had an hour before my Creative Writing class, I went to the computer lab to check my e-mail. I was hoping to hear from Steve Hartley regarding my situation, but there was no message from him yet. As I thought about that situation, I realized that after I opened up and told him the truth about everything, I rarely thought about it again. Sure, the situation popped into my head once in a while, but I didn't dwell on it. And then I realized that Megan hadn't asked me about it on Saturday either. Prior to our date, I thought for sure she would bring it up, but she never did. Oh well. I would find out soon enough and move on.

As we entered the classroom, I could feel a bit of a buzz in the air. People were getting more and more excited about the films with each class. This is an obvious exaggeration, but I compared it to all the celebrities walking the red carpet before the Oscar ceremonies. And then, a celebrity appeared: Doreen. I forgot she was coming, and I forgot to mention that possibility to Ms. Cavellari beforehand, but she didn't mind at all. "Bring all your friends if you want; that's great exposure for this course and for our film festival if we ever get it off the ground."

Doreen had walked over from the dorm with Megan, and I began to wonder about their conversation. Did they talk about me? Would Doreen be upset that I took Megan to dinner and a movie? Would they negotiate over me? I could just imagine that conversation:

"Do you want him?"

"Not really? Do you?"

"I'm not sure."

Fortunately, I didn't have much time to worry about it because Ms. Cavellari asked me if I wanted to go first.

"Sure," I replied.

"Okay, why don't you introduce your film, and, if you'd like, tell us a little bit about it."

"Well, the film is called "Shadows," and I think I will let the film speak for itself."

We turned the lights down. The film began with a sunrise behind the dome of the main classroom building at the college. Then, with an early-morning nature soundtrack, the viewers walk with the photographer from that building to the dorm where Doreen lives. The viewers don't see any people, however; all they see are the shadows of students walking from one building to another.

Upon arriving at the dorm, the scene shifts to Doreen and to her room in the dormitory. She is just preparing to leave. She combs her hair one last time, she grabs her purse, she steps into her shoes, and just before she exits the room, she pauses to look in the mirror. "You can do this," she tells herself. "You can do this."

The next scene occurs at the mall, and it looks like Doreen is about to enter the jewelry store, but again, she pauses and turns around. She retreats to The Donut Shop where she purchases a small coffee. I may have overdone the shot of all the money in her wallet, but I'll have to wait and see what my classmates say later. Instead of sitting in one of the small booths, she stands at one of the high tables, takes a few long sips, and marches back to the jewelry store. Her lips are moving. I'm hoping the audience will be able to see that again she is saying, "You can do this. You can do this. You can do this."

Then came what I think is the best part of the film. I used the security view of Doreen entering the store and browsing at the front counter. The scene looks so real because it's in black and white, and the viewer has to keep looking for her in the midst of all the other customers. We can see her trying on different bracelets and looking at all the different earrings. Then, she used the trick she learned from Tony; she pretended to get a cell-phone call, and just before she left the store, she returned the pair of earrings to the small rack. She held the cell phone in her right hand, and she kept the stolen bracelet, with the price tag, on her left hand, which was completely hidden by the sleeve of her jacket.

As she exits the store, the view shifts back to color, and the viewer can see a serious look on her face, a look that gradually turns into a grin and then a smile as she moves farther and farther from the store. Her goal and her victory have been achieved.

Then, I used one of the oldest filming tricks in the book. To show the passage of some time, I had Doreen walk outside the mall to smoke a cigarette. Since Doreen has never smoked one in her life, I simply had her fumble in her purse, pull one up, and appear to light it. Then, I shifted to the shadow of her silhouette, and fortunately, the air was cold enough that day that when she breathed out, her shadow made it appear as if she were really smoking. After I filmed her crushing a third cigarette, she took off the stolen bracelet, threw it in the trash, and entered the mall again.

This time, Doreen approached the fancy toy store, and as she gathered her courage, I showed all of the ridiculous things they have in there such as an automatic watch winder ($200, and who even wears a watch these days, much less one that has to be wound?), a laser star projector (also $200), and an electric opener for a wine bottle (only $50). Mr. Chips greeted her when she entered, and their conversation revealed her intentions.

"Good afternoon, my lady, and how are you on this gorgeous fall day?"

"I'm well, thank you. Do you mind if I look around while I wait for my boyfriend?"

"He's a lucky man, whoever he is. Please feel free to browse."

Doreen appeared much more nervous here, and I focused on her face quite a bit as she kept looking to see where Mr. Chips was and what he was doing. He didn't seem to suspect her at all, so when another customer finally entered, he became fully engaged in a conversation, and Doreen quickly and efficiently dropped the pen-and-pencil set into her purse. Then, slowly, she looked at a few more items before she exited. Rather than film her face this time, though, I showed her from behind as she walked down the hall. Viewers could see her walk change to a slight skip, and she thrust both hands in the air just like Mark Sanchez does when he throws a touchdown pass.

In both of the theft scenes, I used tense, dramatic music for the actual shoplifting and switched it to upbeat, celebratory music when she succeeded. That music continued into the next scene in her dorm room where she pulls out the pen and in big, bold letters writes "I did it!" The music changes, though, when Doreen can't bring herself to actually leave the pen and the pencil on her desk. Viewers see her shaking her head from side to side as she considers what she's done. Soon, she is leaving again to return to the mall.

When she enters the store a second time, Mr. Chips is busy with another customer, so Doreen rushes a bit too quickly to the display case. Thinking that the coast is clear, she reaches into her purse, but before she can remove the gift box, Mr. Chips has pounced on her. He grabbed her empty hand, and, then, he also reached into her purse to remove the gift box. "Do you have a receipt for that, young lady?"

Surprised by how quickly he got to her, she fumbled for words. He was visibly enraged at that point, probably because he had mistakenly trusted her earlier in the day. I decided to use the cut where he screamed at her in front of everyone before he handed her over to security. My seven-minute movie ended with Doreen being escorted out of the mall and led into a waiting police car. As the funeral music played and as the car drove off, I focused on the car's shadow rather than the car itself.

While all the previous movies received a nominal round of applause from the students, this one received nothing but silence for a few seconds before the class actually gave it a standing ovation. I was stunned.

"Tom, that was phenomenal," Ms. Cavellari gushed, "and your actress, please tell me her name again."

"Doreen."

"Doreen, thank you. That was a remarkable performance, just remarkable. Class, please tell Tom and Doreen what you liked about their movie before we ask them any questions."

The comments came quickly.

"I loved the shadows and the music."

"Getting that scene in the jewelry store on the security camera was a touch of genius. Great job. The contrast between color and black and white really worked well."

"I wasn't sure why you showed us her wallet early on, but I think I get it now."

At that point, I jumped in to ask if I overplayed that scene, and no one had a problem with it. Our discussion went for a full 20 minutes, and Doreen actually got more questions than I did. To her credit, she handled them well, and she kept telling everyone what a great job I did explaining what I wanted. She really raved about the final product which she had never seen before.

The key topic of conversation was the shadows, and most people picked up on the idea that Doreen's character wasn't who she appeared to be. She wasn't shoplifting out of need but because of other reasons which were not obvious on the surface.

People also commented quite a bit on her attempt to return the stolen property. Some thought she truly felt remorse, and others felt she really wanted to get caught. I explained that I was trying to convey remorse and a desire to make things right, but as I watched Doreen's performance, I could also see why some people saw a different motivation for returning to the store. One girl even expressed that Mr. Chips played a symbolic role in the film, a father figure and her desire to be disciplined by him. That idea never crossed mind as I was filming.

Even though the discussion was still going strong, Ms. Cavellari said we had to move on to another film, so we could devote a fair amount of discussion time to that film as well. Immediately, Megan volunteered, and she offered a brief introduction.

"Just as Tom and Doreen worked together on their film, Tom and I also collaborated in a way."

"We did?" I asked myself silently.

"After Tom told me about his idea for his film, I, too, decided to explore a similar subject but in a different way."

I gave Megan a funny look, so when she passed me on her way to the front of the room, she leaned over and whispered, "Just go along with everything I say, and I'll explain later."

"Okay."

I didn't have a clue what she was talking about, but I found out soon enough. She called her film "Just Desserts," and when it opened, I couldn't believe what I saw. The scene was filmed right here in this classroom, and there I was on the screen. Apparently, Megan had filmed me in secret just as she did on the cruise. I was sitting at my computer, writing. Then, she filmed Ms. Cavellari walking into the room and walking up to the desk and preparing to log in. I knew what was coming next, and sure enough, the film zoomed in on her computer monitor which was projected up on the screen. I felt like I was re-living my life. Ms. Cavellari logged in with her user name, and without the cursor moving, she also typed her password, which showed up for everyone to see. Obviously, Megan hadn't filmed the actual mistake; she re-created the scene based on what I had told her, and, quite honestly, she did a great job. If I didn't know the truth, I would have believed that what I was seeing was filmed as it happened. I knew it was a re-creation, though, because I had never told Megan the password, so she created one for her film. Instead of "GoPats2002," Megan used "BostonGirl2010."

Then, she filmed me looking at the screen and hastily writing something in my notebook. As I watched the subsequent scenes, I couldn't believe Megan had filmed me so often without me knowing. Of course, I shouldn't have been so surprised; those Flip cameras are so small, about the size of a cell phone, that it's easy to film discreetly.

I couldn't tell where she was going with the film, but she did a great job of shooting all those computer scenes; she had numerous shots of me working at the computer in the classroom and in the computer lab in the library. She even had one of me working on my laptop in the lounge outside the cafeteria. Boy, if she didn't make it as a filmmaker, she definitely had a future in espionage. She interspersed all those shots of me working on computers with fabricated shots that made it look like I was reading Ms. Cavellari's e-mails and looking in her folders and files and her Facebook account.

At that point, I looked around at my classmates to see their reactions, and they all seemed a little tense, like they couldn't tell if this really happened or if Megan and I simply created the whole thing. Ms. Cavellari looked a little tense too, and I was feeling as nervous as anyone else. From that perspective alone, I guess I'd have to say that Megan's film work was phenomenal, and I was also as eager as everyone else to see what would happen.

Next, Megan showed me, ostensibly, reading specific e-mails from both Tony Masterson and Ricardo to Ms. Cavellari, one inviting her to the cruise and the other asking about when he can come to visit her. After that, the viewers saw me doing a Google search on Ricardo and later typing an e-mail to him and telling him about the cruise. This time, however, it looked not like an accidental forward from Ms. Cavellari but like an intentional and anonymous message from me to let Ricardo know what was going on, as if I were trying to provoke a confrontation. I think everybody knew what was going to happen next, and Megan didn't disappoint.

She used the fight scene from the cruise, and the guys in the class were all pumped up and cheering as they watched me put Ricardo in a headlock. I was pretty pumped myself. When I viewed the fight previously, I saw it on the small screen of the camera, and now I was watching it on the big screen in the classroom. I really was bigger than life, and I was enjoying it. My excitement, however, was tempered by what followed.

The next few scenes showed me receiving the e-mail from Steve Hartley, meeting him in the hallway in the Computer Services Building, and sitting down with him in that classroom. How did she get those scenes with Steve Hartley? I hadn't told her when or where the meeting was to take place. Obviously, she didn't show the entire conversation because that would have taken too long, but she did show all the key points, especially the part where I confessed everything. I was really intrigued by what I saw, and I began to wonder about what the viewers were thinking. Did they assume that this whole thing was staged and that I was a great actor? Or did they assume that what they were viewing was real, and that I was, indeed, guilty of all they had seen on the screen?

Fortunately, the movie ended soon, and just as the viewers read Steve Hartley's final e-mail to me, I read his decision as well.

"Tom,

The Student Senate, the Vice President for Student Affairs, and I have all reviewed your situation, and we are in agreement regarding your punishment. You will be placed on behavior probation for the remainder of this school year. If you stay out of trouble during that time and maintain your good academic standing, that probation will be removed from your college record. If you have any questions about this decision, please contact me.

Steve Hartley"

When the lights came up, Megan and I made eye contact, and the class applauded for the film. Immediately, Ms. Cavellari addressed me somewhat apprehensively and complimented me for my performance on the screen. "Tom, not only are you great behind the camera, but you are also pretty good in the front of the camera." I think she, too, was in doubt about what she had just seen: true documentary or fictional portrayal based on some real events. She continued: "Do you wish to say anything about this film?"

Since I wasn't quite sure how Megan was going to play it, I deferred to her: "I don't mind answering questions, but I think you should hear from the director first."

Megan smiled at my answer and jumped right in. "As most of you know, I happened to have my camera the night of the altercation on the river cruise, so I decided I had to use that somehow. Initially, when I mentioned the idea to Tom, he didn't think it was such a good idea, but because I was struggling to come up with anything else, he decided to help me out. So, we brainstormed ideas about how that situation came about, and this is what we came up with."

"So who was that guy playing Steve Hartley?" Tom Adomat asked. "I work part-time for Steve, so I know that wasn't him." I wanted to know the answer to that question myself.

"Oh, that's my brother Larry," Megan said with a laugh. "He loves to act, so when I ran the idea by him, he was all for it. I suppose I could have used a student actor, but I wanted someone who looked older to make it more believable."

Then, another student asked Megan a question: "You said earlier that you and Tom worked together on your films; was having a similar theme always in your plan, or did it just happen?"

"It really just happened. We were still brainstorming ideas for my film when Tom showed me a first draft of his. I liked the idea of Doreen trying to make things right because she felt guilty, and I also liked the idea of a character coming clean not on his own but only when pushed to the edge by those in authority. If Tom's character hadn't been cornered, he never would have admitted his mistake. After we talked it over, Tom and I both agreed that these were the two extreme positions for those people who make these kinds of mistakes."

Megan was on a roll now, lying her way through this experience and, in some ways, putting on a better performance than Doreen had in my film. I knew we would have to talk later about everything that had happened, and I wasn't sure how I felt about what she had done to me. Should I be upset because she set me up? Or should I be relieved that she was covering for me now? And if Steve Hartley was really Megan's brother, where did I stand in terms of what I had done. Did anybody besides Megan and me really know anything?

My thoughts were interrupted when Ms. Cavellari came back at me with a question: "Tom, since, as I mentioned before, you were on both sides of the camera for this project, which one did you find more difficult, and which one did you find more satisfying?"

I still had a feeling she was fishing for something, but if Megan could pull it off, so could I, especially since everyone in the class already assumed I was a great actor.

"Even though I was a little nervous, I definitely feel the acting part was easier, and the directing part was more difficult. With the acting, I pretty much just followed Megan's directions, and once we filmed the scenes, I was done. But as the director, I spent so much more time putting together all the scenes and finding the right music and special effects and everything else. It was a ton of work."

"Okay, we're just about out of time," said Ms. Cavellari, "but since we saw two great films today, let's do a quick vote to see which one you felt was stronger. Who votes for Megan's film?" About half the hands went up in the air. "And who votes for Tom?" Not surprisingly, the other half of the class raised their hands.

"Okay, it looks like we have a tie. Megan and Tom, congratulations to you both."

When the class ended, Doreen said she had to meet with one of her teachers, so she congratulated us, said she'd talk to us later, thanked Ms. Cavellari for allowing her to visit the class, and, then, disappeared.

Both Megan and I hung around as everyone else left the classroom, and just about everyone gave one of us or both of us a compliment on our work. That was wonderful, of course, but I wasn't sure what was going to happen next. So we silently left the building together, and once we got outside, I spoke.

"So what was that all about?"

"Tom, please don't be mad at me."

"Well, obviously, it turned out well for both of us, but I need to understand what was going on there."

"Oh, all right. At first, I was really mad at you for what you did to Ms. Cavellari. It seemed like you just viewed it like a harmless prank, and you were only worried about how it would affect you."

"And that bothered you why?"

"Because I'm a woman, and the world is filled with crazy sickos who do stupid stuff like stalking women and harassing them and all kinds of other things that I don't even want to mention."

"And you think I'm in that category?"

"No, not at all. I like you, Tom; I like you a lot. I just felt like you had violated her, and you didn't seem to care that much."

"You didn't seem to be that concerned when I first told you about it."

"Can we sit down somewhere to talk about this? Somewhere quiet and private?"

We were passing by the science building at that moment, so I suggested we go inside and find a deserted spot somewhere. Since most of the students were heading up the staircase, I ushered us downstairs, and we found some lounge chairs outside a pair of rest rooms. Once we got settled, and once the few passersby had left us alone, she spoke again.

"You're right about my initial reaction; you're absolutely right. You told me about it that night on the boat, and I don't think I had fully processed all of my ideas. I had just filmed you fighting with Ricardo, we were all hanging out together – you, me, Doreen, and even Ms. Cavellari and Mr. Masterson – and I think I was overwhelmed; information overload, I think they call it? When I went home that night and thought about it, and when I thought about it the next day, too, I became more and more bothered by it, and I was even a little upset with myself for being so flip about it. I remember you asked 'What happened to my helpful psychologist,' and I simply said, 'You need more than a psychologist.'"

"So you decided to get even with me without talking to me about it."

"I did, and I'm sorry; I shouldn't have done that. I should have come to you; I know that now. Can you forgive me? I'm really sorry. I am."

"It just doesn't seem like you. I always thought you were a bit more rational, less emotional than most girls. Was I wrong?"

"I think there was one other factor that really pushed me over the edge."

"And that factor was?"

"Once I saw how good that film was of the fight, I became selfish and self-centered on top of being self-righteous."

I was speechless at that point, and since Megan could probably tell by the look on my face that I was confused, she continued.

"Since I didn't have a strong idea for my film when we boarded that ship, and since I was still experimenting with the camera, I knew I had to use that clip somehow, and I felt it would make a great exposé."

"So, your original intent was to expose me as . . . as what?"

"I don't know . . . maybe just a careless and clueless male who thought he was playing a harmless prank on someone."

"So you were going to prank me in return. You were going to 'punk' me; isn't that what they call it?"

"Something like that."

"So why the change of heart? Why did you make such a big deal today about us working together? Why not just go ahead and make me out to be a fool?"

"Because you redeemed yourself, Tom Sullivan. You proved to me that you were a man. You made me look like the fool for doubting you."

"What did you expect me to do?"

"Well, if you remember, you told me earlier that you wanted to tell Ms. Cavellari the truth, but that you didn't think you could. And even after that, you said your computer friend said they'd never find you, so I guess I thought it was up to me to take a stand for all of womankind and teach you a lesson."

"So you thought I was going to lie about it?"

"I didn't think you would out and out lie, but I thought you might just try and play stupid or simply do what you could to avoid having the truth come out, like maybe plead the Fifth Amendment like all the real criminals do and make Computer Services come forward with some actual proof."

At that point, I became silent and reflective. To her credit, Megan just waited for me to speak. Should I admit to her that I did consider playing stupid or stonewalling or even lying, anything to save myself from detection and punishment? As I thought about all this, I realized that despite what Megan had said in class about the two extreme ways of dealing with guilt, my abrupt confession was just like Doreen's character's attempt to undo what she had done. Yes, I had been pushed to that point, but I could have gone further, and I didn't. I, too, wanted to correct my mistake and be done with it, even if I had to pay a price.

"You're probably right."

"About what?"

"Mostly everything. From the very beginning, I knew what I was doing was wrong. I didn't tell anybody about it – not even my roommate – and whenever I went into her account, I always made sure I was alone or at least somewhat isolated, so no one would be able to see what I was doing."

"But you did it anyway?"

"I did. I couldn't resist, at least not for long. The temptation was so strong, and the situation was so easy. Nobody knew but me."

"And because it was Ms. Cavellari . . . ?" and Megan just let that question hang in the air.

"Busted."

Again, there was a long silence between us. Real long. I think she was waiting for me to say I'd forgive her, and I wasn't there yet. This time, I needed to process what had just happened.

"So what happens next?" I finally said.

"It's your call, I guess."

"I think I need some time."

"Fair enough." She stood to go and appeared to hesitate.

"What?" I asked.

"Can we at least talk again when we get back from Thanksgiving break?"

"Sure."

So, she took off, and I sat there thinking for a long time – about a lot of things. I thought, first, about my relationship with her. She obviously went behind my back and tricked me and had set out to humiliate me. Yes, she had apologized for all of that, but could I ever trust her again? She was the one person I had trusted. If Frankie or Teddy had turned me in, I would have been less surprised. But Megan. I didn't see that coming at all.

Next, I thought about Doreen. Would she ever do something like that to me? Would she betray me and try to make me look bad? I didn't think so, but, obviously, I was wrong about Megan, so I could be wrong about Doreen too. In any event, did Megan's error automatically shift my decision in Doreen's favor? Believe it or not, the situation made me think about starting quarterbacks. When a coach can't decide who should start, an injury to one often makes the decision easier, but that doesn't necessarily mean it's the right decision. So when I finally forgive Megan, and I'm sure I will, what do I do then if I've already made my decision for Doreen? No wonder those coaches make the big bucks.

Finally, I had to think about the whole computer situation all over again. I thought I was done with it because of my confession to Steve Hartley, but I didn't actually confess to the real Steve Hartley. So what should I do next? I could go back to my do-nothing plan and wait for something to happen. Or, I could be, as Megan said, "a man" and confess everything to both Ms. Cavellari and to Computer Services. Or maybe I could find some kind of a compromise plan between those options. And what about Ricardo? If I did actually confess everything, did he deserve a confession and an apology as well? I was completely stumped, I have to admit.

Since I didn't know what to do, I did what I always do when I can't make up my mind about something: I get something to eat, and, then, I take a long nap. So I walked alone to the cafeteria, I ate alone while reading the newspaper, and I walked alone back to the dorm. There, I set down my books, took off my sneakers, climbed into bed, pulled the covers up to my neck, and settled in for a restful snooze.

When I awoke about four hours later, I felt like I wanted to see Doreen, so I texted her and asked her if she wanted to have supper together in the cafeteria. She texted back that she could meet me there at 5:30. So I washed my face, brushed my teeth, put on a shirt that wasn't wrinkled, and headed over.

"Hi Tom," she said when she saw me waiting outside. "I am so sorry I had to leave early today. We have so much to talk about."

That's a good sign, I thought as we entered.

"What teacher did you have to see?"

"My business teacher. I'm on the edge between a B and an A, so I want to make sure that I finish strong in there to actually get the A."

"That's perfectly understandable."

"I know, but I wanted to hang around with you and Megan and talk about your films over lunch. It seemed like everybody really liked both films. I know I did. And I can't believe neither one of you ever told me that you were going to be in Megan's film."

"But didn't you know she was going to use the fight scene?"

"Well, yes, she did tell me about that, but otherwise, she only told me that she was struggling to put the rest together and that she wasn't even sure about her main idea. So, quite honestly, I didn't expect her film to be that good. And I had no idea you were such a good actor. Have you acted before?"

"I had a real small part in a St. Patrick's Day play in eighth grade."

"That's it?"

"That's all."

"Wow! You were pretty awesome. That scene with the computer guy was so believable."

"Yeah."

By that point in the conversation, we had both filled our trays with turkey and mashed potatoes, and stuffing and cranberry sauce, and we were looking for a place to sit.

"Isn't it so cool," Doreen said as she walked, "that the College gives us a Thanksgiving meal before we head home to do the same thing with our family? I love this school." Then, she said a quick "Hello" to some friends and led us to a deserted table in the far corner, a perfect spot for a romantic conversation.

"You got a lot of compliments about your acting, you know," I said as we began to eat.

"Really? Tell me everything."

So I told her about some of the general comments – "great, awesome, phenomenal" – and, then, I mentioned how Dave Botch, who is in the Drama Club, said he'd really like to talk to her about being in their spring production.

Doreen was bubbling over. "Oh, my God! Isn't that what I told you I wanted to do? This is so great. Tom, when we leave here, you have to make sure you send me a copy of that film by e-mail, so I can show my parents when I get home. My mom is going to flip when she sees me acting again."

I wasn't sure where the conversation should go next, so I waited for her to lead.

"And wouldn't that be so cool if Ms. Cavellari really sets up the film festival, so everyone can see what we did!"

We had another short pause before Doreen redirected the conversation. "So tell me, why didn't you say something earlier about being in Megan's film?" I sensed a bit of an edge in the tone of her question.

"Are you mad about that?"

"I guess I'm a little disappointed."

"With Megan, too?"

"Yeah. I thought the three of us were all in this together, especially after the river cruise. Are you two dating or something?"

"No, we're just friends."

"So . . . ?"

"So the truth is I didn't know about that computer scene myself, and Megan secretly filmed all of the other scenes, too, in addition to the fight scene."

"What?"

So I explained everything to Doreen: from the accidental discovery of Ms. Cavellari's password to the long conversation that Megan and I had earlier that day after class. Doreen was stunned into silence.

I gave her a short while to process before I asked, "So Megan hadn't told you about any of this?"

"No."

"The whole thing was stupid on my part, but now, maybe you can see what I was trying to work out in my film."

"Wow!"

"What?"

"It all makes sense now. When you were explaining things to me before we filmed those scenes, you seemed so intense, and once or twice, I asked myself 'What is he dealing with?' I wanted to believe that you just had great insights into human nature, but I also considered the possibility that you had some dark, painful secret that you were trying to exorcise."

"So why didn't you ask?"

"Would you have told me the truth then?"

"I don't know . . . . Probably not."

We had both stopped eating, and she was pushing her remaining mashed potatoes into her cranberry sauce. Then, she broke the silence with a question: "How do you feel about what Megan did to you?"

"Quite honestly, I'm still trying to figure that out."

"In some ways, I think what Megan did to you is worse than what you did to Ms. Cavellari."

"Tell me why."

"In your case, Ms. Cavellari had no idea what was going on, right?"

"Right."

"In Megan's case, you also didn't know what was going on, so that's the same, but her plan was to use your ignorance against you. She was really trying to hurt you and punish you for what she felt you had done wrong."

"Yeah, but I think I was also trying to hurt or punish Ricardo in some way."

"Whose side are you on here?"

"I'm just saying . . . ."

"Okay, I guess you both crossed the line, but what would have happened if you had not confessed, if Megan had felt your 'performance' in her film had not been satisfactory? If you had lied or played stupid, would she still have gone ahead and shown the film? Of course she would; she had nothing else to show. But would she have presented it as a documentary, an exposé of your mistakes, or would she have said the whole thing was fictional and let you off the hook? I'm guessing she would have embarrassed you in front of all your classmates."

"Whatever."

"You do have a right to be angry with her. I know I am."

Doreen was inching far ahead of Megan by the second, and I felt this was a good time to make my move.

"Alright, can I change the subject here for a second?"

"Let me get some pie first; do you want any?"

"Sure."

"Apple or pumpkin?"

"Apple."

When she returned, the slices of pie in her hands seemed to have restored some of her sweetness.

"Okay, what's up?" she asked.

"Doreen, I have really enjoyed getting to know you these past few weeks." She stopped eating and looked me straight in the eye. I continued. "When you get back from break, may I take you out on an actual date?"

"You're serious, aren't you?"

"Is that a problem?"

"Tom, I think you're a great guy, but . . . but I don't see us going in that direction."

"Is it because of everything I just told you?"

"No."

"So?"

"I don't know how to explain it."

"Do you already have a boyfriend back home?"

"Sort of."

"What does that mean?"

"Well, you know how you have this thing for Ms. Cavellari?"

"Yeah."

"So I have this thing for the older brother of one of my best friends."

"And?"

"And I think in some ways, he still sees me as a little kid, but I've seen enough positive signs that I feel like something could happen, maybe even this weekend. So I don't want to give you any false hope. Let's just keep our relationship as director and actress. We're pretty good together, you know."

"Yeah, alright."

"Seriously, let's at least stay friends."

"I feel a movie coming on."

She laughed.

And I cried all the way back to my dorm. Not really. I was disappointed, but I maintained my composure. I walked her to her dorm, I gave her a hug, and she gave me a harmless peck on the cheek. I was a coach without a quarterback again.

Did I consider Megan again? Of course I did. But not for long. I think Doreen was right; Megan could have hurt me bad. It didn't turn out that way, but it could have happened. So I tried to put the two of them behind me, and I began thinking about spending Thanksgiving at home with my family. Would I show them the film? I wasn't sure. They might have too many questions, and I know I didn't yet have all the right answers.

Unfortunately, I was also pondering the two questions I had asked myself previously. Should I come clean to Ms. Cavellari, and should I come clean with Computer Services? The only real decision I had made was that I would never come clean with Ricardo. He was too much of a nut case, and I don't even think he would ever understand. All he knows is that I had him in a headlock, and I'm sure he'd want to return the favor. So as I walked into my dorm, I tried to convince myself that I should confess to both Ms. Cavellari and to the real Steve Hartley before I went home for the holiday. I had a strong feeling that the conversation with Ms. Cavellari would be much more difficult, but I also felt that she would be much more understanding and much more forgiving.

Tuesday, November 23

This morning, I sat through my 8:00 science class and, then, headed over to Ms. Cavellari's office because I knew she had a 9:00 office hour. When I arrived, however, she was just settling in, and three other students were already in line to see her. "Tom," she said when she saw me, "I might not get to you this hour, but I have another office hour at eleven o'clock if you can come back."

"I'll do that."

Since I didn't have a class to go to at that moment, I knew what I had to do next: visit Computer Services. I was hoping to clear things up with Ms. Cavellari before I spoke to Steve Hartley, but since she wasn't available, I felt like fate was telling me to reverse the order of my appointments. So onward I went.

When I arrived at the Computer Services Building, I walked down the same hallway I had used the previous week. I half expected to see Megan's brother there waiting for me. This time, however, I actually entered the office and asked for Steve Hartley.

"Who may I say is here, and what is the purpose of the visit?"

"My name is Tom Sullivan, and I'd like to report a computer problem."

"You can fill out a form and just leave it for Steve if you'd like."

"No, that's okay; I'd like to speak to him in person if that's okay; I can wait if I have to."

"You may take a seat right there."

As I waited, I replayed my confession in my mind, and I prepared myself for the worst.

About ten minutes later, I was sitting in front of Steve Hartley, and he was about 30 years older and 20 pounds heavier than Megan's brother. Like Megan's brother, though, Steve was very friendly and professional.

"Tom, what can I do for you?"

"I'd like to turn myself in for a computer infraction, and I hope you will show me some mercy for my honesty."

"Pardon me?"

"I know it's pretty unusual, but here's what happened."

Then, I told him the story pretty much the same way I had told Doreen. I left out some of the touchy, feely stuff behind my motivations, and unlike Doreen, he listened to the whole confession without asking any questions. When I finished, I again pleaded for mercy, and he only paused for about three seconds before he responded.

"So you're the guy."

This time, it was my turn to say, "Pardon me?"

"Ms. Cavellari was in last week, sitting in that same chair, in fact, and she reported her suspicion that someone had compromised her computer account. She said she had changed her password, but she was worried that whoever had done this to her might also be able to see the change."

"Did she mention my name as a possible suspect?"

"She did not. In fact, she seemed to imply that someone outside the college might be the culprit, an 'old boyfriend,' I believe she said."

"What did you tell her?"

"I told her that under the circumstances, it would take us quite a while to find the person, but eventually, we would dig up the information. I also told her the process would be even longer than normal because of the upcoming Thanksgiving weekend. She understood, and I let her know that I would get back to her as soon as I had any information. So now – "

"I'm sorry to interrupt, but if it's okay with you, I'd like to tell her myself rather than have you inform her."

"And why is that?"

"Because I feel pretty bad about what I did, and I'd rather she hear it directly from me."

"How do I know you will follow through?"

"You don't. I have an appointment to see her at eleven o'clock this morning, though, so you can call her any time after eleven to see if I did follow through."

"That part sounds okay." He paused for a long time, then, and I waited until he spoke again. "I'm not sure what to do about your punishment, however."

"I'd be willing to work for you to pay off my debt. I could help in one of the computer labs; I could carry stuff around campus for you; I'd do whatever you asked."

"I like what I'm hearing, Tom, but I can't make a final decision until after you explain everything to Ms. Cavellari and after I speak to her. If she wants to pursue this case, it could go to the Senate Judiciary Board, but if she drops it, we'll be all done."

"Okay."

"So, we'll talk again after you finish talking with Ms. Cavellari."

"Alright. Thank you."

I still had time to kill, so, believe it or not, I walked over to the church on campus. I knew the place would be empty, and no one would bother me. I knew what I was going to say to Ms. Cavellari because I had gotten pretty good at telling this particular story, but I felt like I needed some extra help. Yes, I needed to pray.

Quite honestly, I don't pray that often. I usually save it for desperate causes only. I used to bother God with every little concern on my mind, and for a while, I really got carried away. I was actually praying every time the Jets had a game, and I knew that wasn't right. As a result, I think I went to the other extreme. On this particular day, though, I wanted His help. Not that I was all that worried about any punishment that the school might give me. I was much more concerned about what Ms. Cavellari would think of me. Despite what Megan had done to me personally, she did make me realize that what I had done to Ms. Cavellari was much more than a prank or a joke. I had violated her trust in me, and I wanted to try and regain it. So I told God everything that was on my mind, and after I was done, I felt much better about approaching her with my apology.

Ms. Cavellari and I arrived at her office building at about the same time, so I held the door open for her and asked if I could carry her bag up the stairs.

"Well, aren't you the gentleman! Thank you."

She made small talk while we climbed the stairs, walked down the hall, and entered her office. "Please have a seat," she said as she took off her coat and hung it on a nearby coat rack. "What's on your mind?"

"I owe you an apology," I said immediately. "I'm sorry."

"For what?"

And for the third time within the last day or so, I confessed. Once again, it was the same basic story, but I apologized early and often during this version of the story. When I described how she had accidentally revealed her password three weeks earlier, she did remember the incident happening, but she said she didn't think anyone had noticed. Megan's film, though, reminded her of that day, so she knew she wanted to ask me about it.

Later, when I mentioned how I had read her e-mails and looked at her pictures, she lost that beautiful smile and her friendly demeanor. She just kept staring at me in disbelief. I felt terrible, but I continued. And, finally, when I explained that it was my fault that Ricardo was in Troy the night of the cruise, she lost it and began crying silently. I knew I couldn't hug her or comfort her, so I kept apologizing and trying to explain.

"I know it was none of my business, but I just knew that Ricardo was not right for you. You deserve better. You're too good for him. I was mad at Ricardo. I was jealous of Mr. Masterson for asking you out. And I was angry at you for being so nice and sweet to everyone. I wanted you to stand up for yourself, so they wouldn't hurt you, and when you didn't, I got carried away. Again, I'm sorry. I know what I did was wrong and stupid and way out of line, especially intruding in your private affairs, but once I knew what was going on, I wanted to help. I really did. I was just stupid and immature, and I'm sorry. I hope you'll forgive me, but I'll completely understand if you don't."

She was still sobbing a little, and I was out of apologies. I probably should have left at that point, but I was hoping she would say something, so I waited. Then, the phone rang. I assumed it had to be Steve Hartley. She let it ring three times while she composed herself before she picked it up.

"Good morning, this is Margaret Cavellari . . . . Yes, Steve. Thank you for getting back to me . . . . Yes, he is here . . . . Yes, he did . . . . Really?"

The tone of her voice was starting to change, becoming a bit more upbeat, like the Margaret of old. I was becoming a bit more upbeat myself.

"So what do you think I should do?" She asked next. "Is there a standard procedure for this kind of thing? . . . I see . . . . Okay. I think he and I will continue talking, and I will let you know what I decide."

When she hung up, she had definitely recovered somewhat, but she was still staring at me and, I assumed, trying to figure out what to say. I felt like it took her forever before she spoke: "So you think I'm too – what were the words – 'nice and sweet'?"

My words were coming back to haunt me; I could see it coming.

"Well, I'm not feeling too nice and sweet right now. Tom Sullivan, you said you were angry at me; well, now I'm angry with you. Do you realize I could have you kicked out of school for this?"

"And I would deserve it."

"That's right; you would . . . . So tell me, why should I show you mercy? And tell me something new, something I haven't heard yet."

"Because you are a merciful person."

"How do you know that? And don't tell me you read it in my e-mails."

"No, I see it every day in class. I see it when students explain to you about missing class or not having assignments, and you show them mercy. I see it when you evaluate student writing in class, and no matter how bad it is or how far off the mark the writing is, you still find something positive to say about that student's work. And I saw it that night on the boat. I could tell you didn't really want to be with Mr. Masterson, but you were always kind and polite. And when I saw your face when you recognized Ricardo, I saw something I had never seen before. I'm not sure what it was, but it definitely wasn't nice and sweet. You could easily have yelled at him or lashed out at him, but you didn't – for whatever reason. Maybe you were afraid. Maybe you were embarrassed. I don't know what you were feeling . . . . Whatever it was, you didn't hurt him; I did, and I'm sorry. So you can do whatever you want to me, and I'll understand. I'm guilty as charged."

I stood to leave, and I was halfway out the door before she spoke.

"Tom, wait."

I turned and walked back in; I remained standing.

"I'm going to call Steve Hartley when you leave, and I'm going to officially withdraw my inquiry. He said he would go along with any punishment I felt was justified, so as far as I'm concerned, this never happened, and I will let him know that."

"Okay. Thank you. I really appreciate it. Thank you."

"That means you have to forget it as well. And so does anyone else who knows about it. Am I making myself clear?"

"Absolutely."

"Okay. Now get out of here. And go, and have a wonderful Thanksgiving with your family."

And so I did.

Wednesday, November 24

On the night before Thanksgiving, I went out with all of my old high-school buddies, and we had a great time. Everybody had college stories to tell. I actually had one of my own, but because I gave my word to Ms. Cavellari, I didn't share my story with anyone, not even my family members. Instead, I told my friends and my family about my film project and how everybody liked it and how we might have a film festival on campus. When they asked what my film was about, I simply said the story was about a kleptomaniac.

Thursday, November 25

On Thanksgiving Day, even though I was exhausted and even though I am out of shape, I got up early and ran The Turkey Trot, a five-kilometer race through the streets of downtown Troy. My two brothers and I have been running this race every year for about 12 years, ever since my older brother was a freshman in high school. I think my parents love it more than we do now. They get to sit in their folding chairs and drink coffee and eat doughnuts while they watch us sweat our way toward the finish line. I used to care about my time for the race, but this year, I just wanted to finish.

So as I ran slowly but steadily, I reflected on this novel-in-a-month project, and I have to say it was a pretty good experience. I'm pretty sure I'm the only student in our class who is still writing, and, amazingly, I met my 50,000-word quota well before the end of the month. Obviously, I lucked out in a bad sort of way. I became the protagonist in my own story, and unlike most stories where the protagonist is the good guy, I was the bad guy. Does that make me the protagonist/antagonist? I don't know. What I do know is that I learned to write every day and to write a lot every day. I used to view myself as a sprinter when it came to writing, but now I know I can be a marathon writer if I want to, and I do think I want to. I also learned that interesting experiences can lead to great writing opportunities, so I think I want to be an active writer rather than a writer who hides himself away to discover his muse. I think living will be my muse. Whether that means I write fiction or non-fiction, I'm not sure yet, but I know I'll figure that out when the time comes.

As for Ms. Cavellari, after what she did for me, I'm more in love with her than ever, in a platonic sort of way, if you know what I mean. And if she will allow it, I will keep signing up for her writing courses. I have learned so much from her, and she has really pushed me to do my best work. I feel like I want to do something for her in return, something with equal or greater value. Maybe I can give her something that will really transform her life. Maybe I can convince her to give up on the Patriots and root for the Jets.

The End

The Author . . .

Since January of 2000, Jim LaBate has worked as a writing specialist in The Writing Center at Hudson Valley Community College in Troy, New York.

Originally from Amsterdam, New York, Jim graduated from Saint Mary's Institute and Bishop Scully High School. He earned his bachelor's degree in English from Siena College in Loudonville, New York, and his master's degree, also in English, from The College of Saint Rose in Albany, New York.

Jim has spent his entire career as either a teacher or a writer. He taught physical education as a Peace Corps Volunteer in Golfito, Costa Rica, for two years. He taught high-school English for ten years (one year at Vincentian Institute in Albany, New York, and nine years at Keveny Memorial Academy in Cohoes, New York). Then, he worked for ten years as a writer for Newkirk Products in Albany, New York.

Jim lives in Clifton Park, New York, with his wife, Barbara, and their two daughters: Maria and Katrina.

Let's Go, Gaels – a novella by Jim LaBate – tells the story of one week in the life of a 12-year-old boy. The story takes place in a Catholic school in upstate New York in 1964. As the week begins, the narrator is thinking about a speech he has to give in English class on Friday, a big basketball game on Saturday, and a trip to the movies on Saturday night. During the week, however, something happens that changes his life – and his outlook on life – forever. The event moves him further away from his innocent boyhood and closer to his eventual maturity as a man.

Mickey Mantle Day in Amsterdam – another novella by Jim LaBate – is also about growing up. This particular story focuses on baseball and on baseball's biggest name in the 1950's and the 1960's. The story takes place during the summer of 1963 when Mantle is on the disabled list, recovering from a broken foot. When his car breaks down near the "Rug City," the 12-year-old narrator and his dad stop to help, and Mantle's Amsterdam adventure begins. By the time it ends, 24 hours later, both the narrator and the reader have learned a valuable lesson.

Things I Threw in the River: The Story of One Man's Life – In this novel, the first-person narrator lives near the Mohawk River in upstate New York during the 1950's, '60's, '70's, and '80's. He tells a series of related stories about what he threw into the river and why. The first story concerns an incident that occurs when the narrator is four years old, and the final story occurs in 1988 when he is 37. That final story is the most dramatic of all, takes up 50% of the novel, and is based on a real incident.

Order Form

Please send to the following address:

Name_____

Address_____

City _____ State_____Zip _____

Let's Go, Gaels	$5.95 x _____	copies = _____
Mickey Mantle Day in Amsterdam	$7.95 x _____	copies = _____
Things I Threw in the River	$9.95 x _____	copies = _____
My Teacher's Password	$9.95 x _____	copies = _____
Postage	$2.00 x _____	copies = _____

Subtotal _____

New York residents add appropriate sales tax _____

Total _____

Please enclose a check for your order and mail to:

Mohawk River Press

Mohawk River Press
P.O. Box 4095
Clifton Park, New York 12065-0850
518-383-2254
www.MohawkRiverPress.com